THE PREMONITION

THE PREMONITION

BANANA YOSHIMOTO

Translated from the Japanese
by Asa Yoneda

faber

First published in Japan in 1988 by Kadokawa Shoten Publishing Co., Ltd.
Published in the US in 2023 by Counterpoint
COUNTERPOINT
2560 Ninth Street, Suite 318
Berkeley, CA 94710
www.counterpointpress.com

This edition first published in 2023
by Faber & Faber Limited
The Bindery, 51 Hatton Garden
London EC1N 8HN

Printed and bound in the UK by CPI Group (UK) Ltd, Croydon, CR0 4YY

English translation rights arranged with Banana Yoshimoto through ZIPANGO, S.L. and
Michael Kevin Staley

The right of Banana Yoshimoto to be identified as author of this work has been asserted in
accordance with Section 77 of the Copyright, Designs and Patents Act 1988

A CIP record for this book is available from the British Library

ISBN 978–0–571–38230–9

6 8 10 9 7 5

THE PREMONITION

*

The old house was on a residential street, some distance from the train station. The enormous park it backed onto surrounded it at all times with a wild scent of greenery, and after a rain the air stood as thick as if the entire neighborhood had turned into a jungle, making it hard to breathe.

I spent only a brief time in that house where my aunt lived alone for so long. In retrospect, I can see how special a moment it was—one that had been a long time coming, and would never come again. It makes me feel oddly sentimental to think of those days now. Like a mirage that I suddenly discovered was real, they seem to have been cut adrift from the world outside.

I grieve for the clarity of that time I had with my aunt—how lucky I was to share that space with her during a sliver of time that had appeared only by sheer chance. It was over now, but it had to be. In coming to an end, it had given me something, and only by making my way through was I able to begin to live the rest of my life.

I can see it now: The heavy door made of wood had a cloudy brass knob. The weeds in the neglected garden grew thick and lush, stretching tall among the dying trees, shutting out the sky. Vines carpeted the dark exterior walls, and the windows were patched haphazardly with tape. The dust covering the floor rose and danced translucent in the sunlight before settling again. A comfortable clutter reigned, and dead light bulbs were left in peace. Time had no foothold in that house. Until I turned up, my aunt had lived there quietly on her own, as though asleep, for years.

She taught at a private high school. She was thirty, but single, and had lived alone for a long time. Imagine a reserved, spinster music teacher: in the mornings when she left for work, she was the very picture of one. Each day, she'd dress in a stiff mouse-gray suit, tie her hair back with a plain black elastic, and go on her way through the morning haze, wearing no makeup and a pair of heels of an awkward height. You know the type: a woman who's hopelessly unfashionable in spite of having an otherworldly kind of beauty. I could only suspect she was doing it on purpose; following a guide on how to disguise herself as a music teacher to whom no one would give a second glance. Because once she was home, doing nothing in particular and dressed down in what seemed to be her pajamas, she transformed into an elegant stranger.

My aunt lived the life of an eccentric. As soon as she came home from school, she took off her shoes and socks and changed into her pajamas. Left to her own devices, she would lounge around all day trimming her nails and her split ends. She'd gaze absently out the window for hours, or lie down in the hallway and fall asleep. She left her books open half-read and her laundry in the dryer; she ate when she got hungry, and went to bed when she felt like it. Aside from her bedroom and the kitchen, the house didn't seem to have been cleaned in years, and when I first arrived I spent all night battling the dust and grime to remedy the terrifyingly filthy state of the room my aunt gave me to stay in. Even then she was unconcerned and, instead of helping, spent hours baking a cake to welcome me. Every last thing she did was just as topsy-turvy. By the time I finished cleaning and we sat down to eat the cake, day was starting to light up the sky. It was like that with everything—in that household, none of the usual rules or routines of life seemed to exist.

The reason these things still came across as somehow being virtues, I thought, was because my aunt was beautiful. She had pretty features, but in that sense, there were plenty of people more attractive than her. What made her beautiful to me was more like a specific mood whose tendrils pervaded everything, from the way she moved to the way she passed her days to the fleeting expressions that passed across her face when something happened. The feeling was so stubbornly consistent that it seemed unshakable, like something that would continue, untouched, all the way until the end of the world. It made her seem strangely beautiful no matter what she was doing. The vacant yet bright light she gave off filled the space around her. When she lowered her long eyelashes and rubbed her eyes sleepily, she was as dazzling to me as an angel, and when she sat on the floor with her legs sprawled carelessly in front of her, her slender ankles were as smooth and neat as a marble sculpture's. All of the space within the dilapidated old house seemed to ebb and flow along with her movements.

*

That night, I had called her phone repeatedly, but she never picked up. Worried, I'd headed for her house anyway through the pouring rain. The greenery stood smoky in the dark, and somewhere in the suffocating night air was a hint of lonely freshness. The duffel bag on my shoulder weighed enough to make me stagger, but I walked on determinedly. It was a deep, black night.

Leaving home was what I did when I had things to figure out. I'd take a trip without telling anyone where I was going, or go stay with friends. It always cleared my head, let me see things more clearly. My parents were angry with me the first few times, but by the time I was in high school they'd given up on stopping me, so it wasn't out of character for me to come out on a whim like this, with no warning. The only thing I didn't completely understand was why, this time, I found myself heading to my aunt's house.

She and I weren't close, and only really saw each other at big family gatherings. But for whatever reason, I'd always been very fond of my eccentric aunt, and there was also a small incident from the past that was still a secret just between the two of us.

*

This was back when I was still in elementary school.

The morning of my maternal grandfather's funeral, the sky was the kind of bright, cloudy midwinter sky that seemed to be ready to start snowing at any moment. I remember it clearly. I was under the covers, looking up at its diffuse brightness through the paper screen. The mourning clothes I would wear to the funeral waited on a hanger beside the window.

From time to time, I heard Mom's voice in the hallway catch with tears. She'd been on the phone all morning. I was still too young to understand much about death, but I was saddened by her grief.

Among the calls, though, there'd been one where Mom had raised her voice suddenly before hanging up the receiver.

"Wait, what? Yukino! That's not . . ."

There was a silence before she said to herself, more quietly, "How could she?"

Even half-asleep, I understood immediately that my aunt wouldn't be coming to the funeral.

I'd seen her at the wake the night before. Even then she'd seemed to be on a different wavelength from everyone else. By far the youngest and quietest of Mom's siblings, she'd stood alone throughout—and looked breathtaking the whole time. She must have been in her only mourning outfit. I'd never seen her in formal clothes before. When Mom pointed out the dry-cleaning tag hanging from the hem of her black dress and removed it for her, my aunt didn't seem at all embarrassed, or even smile. She simply lowered her head just a little, painfully slowly.

I'd been standing with my family, watching the line of guests, but my aunt captured my full attention. She had dark circles under her eyes, and her lips were pale, the funereal contrast of white and black making her look see-through like a ghost. A huge heater by the reception table outside the gate was spitting heat into the freezing cold darkness. Its roaring flames lent my aunt's cheeks a vigorous red glow. While everybody else kept busy through their sadness, greeting one another and dabbing at their eyes with handkerchiefs, she alone was still, as if she'd become part of the dark night: empty-handed, adorned with a single strand of pearls, only her eyes shining with strength, reflecting the flames.

She's holding back tears, I thought. She'd been the apple of my grandfather's eye, and had been constantly on his mind, especially after she moved out. My grandparents' home wasn't far from hers, so they must have seen one another regularly. That was about as much as I knew then, but watching her standing there gazing into the night, I could feel the depth of her sadness like it was my own. Yes, it was easy for me to understand my aunt. Although she spoke rarely, the small gestures she made, the direction of her gaze, the way she turned her head—each of these seemed somehow to tell me whether she was glad, bored, angry. It always confused me when Mom and other relatives would talk about her, sounding both loving and baffled, and say, "There's no knowing what's going on in that head of hers." Why couldn't they see? And why was it so obvious to me?

The next moment, my aunt suddenly burst into tears. What began as a few clear drops rolling down her cheeks soon turned to sobs, then full-on weeping. I alone had seen it coming. The people standing around were startled and quickly led her away. But they hadn't been watching. They'd been taken by surprise. I was the only one who had witnessed her. I felt the knowledge as a strange confidence inside me.

All my aunt had told Mom that morning before hanging up the phone was that she was leaving. Mom called her back repeatedly, but she didn't pick up. The funeral went ahead without her, and Mom couldn't reach her for days. Resigned, she said, "She must be on a long trip. I'll try her again in a while."

I'd gone to my aunt's house the day after the funeral, convinced she was still at home. I'm impressed I managed it, given I was only nine years old. But each time Mom waited while the phone rang out before laying down the receiver with a sigh, I felt sure my aunt was there on the other end—she just wasn't picking up. I needed to find out if I was right.

I got on the train straight from school, still carrying my schoolbag. Snow was falling intermittently, and it was a terribly cold evening. My heart beat nervously. I just had to see her. When I arrived at her house, it loomed pitch-black in the twilight, and as I went to ring the doorbell, I became worried she wasn't there after all. I pressed it again and again, like some kind of prayer. Eventually, there was a faint sound behind the door, and I knew she was there, standing wordlessly on the other side.

"It's Yayoi," I said.

The door opened with a clang, and my aunt, looking exhausted, stared down at me in disbelief. Her eyes were puffy and red. I knew she must have been alone in the dark house, crying.

"How did you know?" my aunt said.

With trepidation, I said, "I just did." It was all I could manage to say.

"Come in. Don't tell your mom," she said, giving me a small smile. She was wearing white pajamas. It was my first time visiting her on my own, and the inside of her cluttered house seemed lonely and cold.

She took me to her bedroom upstairs. It must have been the only room in the house with a heater in it. There was also a large black piano. She kicked aside various things on the floor to make space for a cushion.

She said, "Sit here. I'll go get something to drink," and went downstairs. It was sleeting now outside the window, and I could hear the ice hitting the panes. I was astonished by how dark and quietly night seemed to arrive in her neighborhood. I couldn't imagine living all alone in a place like this. I started to feel uneasy. Frankly, I wanted to go home. Except—

My aunt came back up the stairs, saying, "Yayoi, are you okay with Calpico?" and her puffy eyes made me feel so sorry for her that I just nodded and took the cup of hot Calpico she held out to me.

She went and perched on the bed, which was the only place left in the room to sit.

Then, really smiling for the first time, she said, "I just skipped school and stayed in bed." I finally felt myself relax. I didn't know why my aunt had moved out of my grandparents' place to live in a run-down place like this. I felt like now that my grandfather was gone, she was truly alone. And because she was treating me like my own person, even though I was just a kid, there was something I wanted her to know.

"Did your mom say I was on a trip?"

"Yeah."

"Don't tell her I'm still here. I don't want to talk to any grown-ups. I can't handle it. You know what I mean?"

"Yeah."

My aunt was at music college then. Her shelves were laden with books of sheet music, and one stood open on the music stand on the piano. A messy pile of ruled paper was on her desk, lit by a lamp.

"Were you practicing?" I said.

"Nope." She smiled, and looked at the open music. "I just left it out. See how dusty it is?"

She stood up and walked quietly over to the glossy piano. Brushing a layer of dust off the keyboard lid, she opened it and sat down on the chair.

"Shall I play you something?"

The room at nightfall was as quiet as eternity. I nodded, and without looking at the music, she started playing something soft. As soon as she sat in front of the keys, her back seemed to grow tall, and I watched her in profile as her head followed her fingers confidently. The tone of the piano and the sounds of the wind and the sleet outside combined into a strange atmosphere, almost as if I were in some other country. For that moment, I was in a dream. I forgot that my grandfather was gone, that my aunt was grieving, and simply opened myself to the sounds that filled the room.

When the piece was over, my aunt let out a breath and said, "It's been a while since I played." She closed the lid and turned to me with a smile. "Are you hungry? Shall we order something?"

"No, I have to get home. They don't know I'm here," I said.

"Good point," she said, nodding. "Do you know the way back to the station? I'm not dressed."

"Yeah."

I got up. Out in the hallway and down the stairs, the harsh cold seemed to bite into me.

"See you," I said, putting my shoes on. There was so much I'd wanted to say, but once face-to-face with my aunt in her desolate house, I hadn't been able to tell her any of it, and that made me feel terribly discouraged. Still, I'd done my best.

I'd just stepped out of the front door when she called out to me.

"Yayoi," she said, in a quiet voice. It had a kind of echo to it. I turned and looked at her. I could tell she was going stay up all night in her dimly lit room. I felt that by coming here and then leaving again, I was making her even more alone. With the hallway light at her back, her bare feet were the only part of her I could see clearly. There seemed to be a strange light in her eyes. They held back a deep gleam, like she was looking at something in the far distance, like there was something she wanted to say.

"Yayoi," she said with a small smile. "Good seeing you."

"Yeah," I said. I felt pretty sure she understood why I'd come to see her. I waved and left, hurrying back through the freezing dark. When I got home, Mom gave me an earful and demanded to know where I'd been, but I didn't tell. It felt like a secret I had to keep.

*

All these years, I'd kept my memory of that brief visit to my aunt's house safe somewhere deep inside my chest: the distinctive color of the air there, and how even time seemed to slow down in her presence. Now it seemed to come rushing back to me in a rush of nostalgia, more strongly and more vividly than ever.

Soon the white walls of my aunt's house appeared from between the trees, and I could see a light through a window. She was home. I breathed a sigh of relief. I walked up to the house, pushed open the squealing, rusty gate laden with darkly sparkling raindrops, and rang the doorbell. Nervously, I listened to her footsteps approach slowly from inside the house.

Behind the door, she stopped and said, "Who is it?"

"It's me. Yayoi," I said, and the door opened with a clang.

Seeing me, she smiled and said, "It's been a while." I looked at her big, deep, clear eyes and the kindly curve of her pale, even lips, feeling as though I were in a dream.

"Sorry to just turn up. I tried calling," I said, swinging my duffel down onto the floor of the entrance hall.

"Oh, the phone? I heard it ringing, but . . . I didn't want to pick up. Sorry about that," she said, and looked at my bag, laughing. "Come on in. Have you been on a trip somewhere?"

"Kind of. I was wondering if I could stay with you for a while, actually. I won't cause any trouble," I said.

"Oh no, running away?" my aunt murmured, eyes wide. She sounded hesitant, but deep down I was confident—*she won't say no. We've always liked each other.*

". . . Please?" I said, quietly.

"Of course," she said brightly, with a look of innocent surprise. "You know I have the space. Stay as long as you like. But come in, it's raining."

The soft sound of the rain that night, the darkness of the falling dusk. As soon as the door swung shut behind me, I was in a different, quiet space. We walked down the creaking hallway into the kitchen. The figure of my aunt in her white pajamas cast a great shadow on the wall as she put the kettle on the old stove. She didn't ask me why I was there, and the scent of black tea filled the room, and I put my elbows on the table and realized—*I just wanted to be here again.* Suddenly, everything made sense. I was so buoyed and joyful I could have cried, but I was also amazed at myself for feeling like this. *All I had to do was come back.*

Later, for the first time in a very long time, I heard my aunt play the piano. Its tone was soft, and just like I remembered it. At the kitchen window one overcast afternoon, I watched its beautiful music as it flowed from her room upstairs, threaded through the trees in the garden, and slipped away into the gray sky. I never knew until I lived there that sound could sometimes become visible to the eye. But no—the sight somehow felt more familiar. The elegant melody awakened a sweet feeling in me, as if I'd once spent long days just like that, watching sounds, somewhere in the distant past. Listening with eyes closed, I felt as though I were at the bottom of a green ocean. All the world seemed to be lit up by shafts of light. The current moved limpidly, and in it, my troubles skimmed past me like schools of fish barely brushing against my skin. I had a premonition of setting out on a journey and getting lost inside a distant tide as the sun went down, ending up far, far away from where I started.

It was the beginning of summer, and I was nineteen years old.

*

That Sunday, Mom had been outside all morning gardening. As I lay in bed, I heard Dad, who'd been roped in to help, talking loudly, complaining, laughing. Drowsily I thought, *If I get up now, she'll make me help with the garden, too, and then Dad will grab his chance to slip off* . . .

Nearly a week had passed since we'd moved back into our freshly renovated house. I was still adjusting, waking with a start each morning to the unfamiliar ceiling. Smells of new paint and fresh timber permeated the rooms, giving them a standoff-ish air. And I'd felt out of sorts since our move. I couldn't shake the sense that something in me was shifting—something was starting to open up in me.

For whatever reason, I had no memories from my child-hood. Not in my mind, or in photos—nothing.

I knew it was weird. But it was the kind of weird that dif-fused into the day-to-day, and because like everyone I was always moving on into the future, at some point I'd stopped thinking about it.

Our family was me, Mom, Dad, and my brother, Tetsuo, who was barely a year younger than me. We were the picture of a happy middle-class family, like in that Spielberg movie. Dad was a doctor at a big corporation, where he'd met Mom, who was a nurse. Our home was always full of sensible exuberance, and never lacked for things like flowers on the table, homemade jams and pickles, crisply ironed outfits, sets of golf clubs, fine liquors. Mom bustled around the house joyfully, bringing up me and Tetsuo, and Dad protected us with a strong heart full of nothing but devotion. I couldn't have been more fortunate; and yet, from time to time, I couldn't help but think—

It's not just my childhood memories. There's something even more important I'm forgetting.

At dinnertime, with the TV on, my parents would often tell stories from when we were younger. Happy memories of me and Tetsuo: the first time we saw a lion at the zoo; the time I fell and split my lip open, and cried when I saw the blood; how I'd always pick on Tetsuo and make him cry . . . There was no hesitation in their words, not a hint of shadow in their smiles, and sitting there with Tetsuo I'd laugh just as heartily as him.

But in my mind, a light would go off. *Something's missing. There's something else . . .* It might have only been my imagination. Most people forgot their childhood memories. That was totally normal. Even so—when I was outdoors, on nights when the moon shone especially bright, things often felt unbearable. I'd look up to the distant sky and feel the air blowing past me, and sense that I was on the verge of recalling something overwhelmingly familiar. I knew it was there, but as soon as I tried to think about it, it would vanish. It had been like that for as long as I could remember. The doubt had come to weigh even more heavily on me since something that happened at the place we'd lived temporarily while our house was being renovated . . .

"Yayoi! Get up, it's almost noon."

I heard Dad call out, and so I reluctantly got up from my bed and headed downstairs. He was in the entryway changing his sandals for sneakers.

"I can't believe you made me get up just so Mom could have someone else to order around!" I said.

"Hardly. It's almost noon, and I've done my part. You hold the fort for a while," he said, laughing. He always looked younger on Sundays, maybe because of the way he let his hair fall naturally over his forehead.

"Going for a walk?"

"Yep, just sneaking out," he said. He'd gotten into taking walks recently, and we were supposed to be getting a puppy soon that he could take out with him. It was a foreign breed that would get huge when it was full-grown. The whole family was looking forward to it.

I opened the door to the living room and went over to the big window looking out on the garden. Through the glass, I could see Mom at the far end of it, in gardening gloves, transplanting a shrub.

I got the milk out of the refrigerator, microwaved a pastry, and started on a late breakfast. My head was groggy from sleeping too long. At the edge of the kitchen, Tetsuo was sawing at a piece of wood with a look of intense concentration.

"Do you have to make so much noise? What are you doing?" I said, going over to him with my mouth full. He had a stack of planks and a can of paint on top of some newspaper he had laid on the floor, and was loudly sawing away.

"I'm building a doghouse," he said, and motioned at the sawdust-covered sheet of paper by his foot.

I picked up the plans. Surprised at the size of it, I said, "I thought we were getting a puppy!"

"That's how big it's going to get when it grows up," he said, and went back to sawing.

"I guess that's why they say great things come in little packages," I said, laughing.

"You're so smart, Yayoi!" he said, keeping his eyes on his saw, and laughed, too.

I crouched there and watched his hands for a while as they worked in the sunlight.

I really loved my brother. He was an easy person to love. That was just the kind of kid he was. Growing up, we were always incredibly close, and never fought, even though he was a boy and I was a girl. I took him for granted sometimes, but at heart I always admired his pure enthusiasm for the world. He met challenges head-on, fearlessly, and had a natural strength and positivity that stopped him from letting his doubts turn into problems for other people. Even now, in his senior year of high school, when he was preparing to take his college entrance exams, he didn't give us any reason to worry about him. He'd cheerfully gone and bought a mountain of workbooks, and was working his way through them methodically, like he was trying to complete a video game—it seemed like a given that he'd get into a college that was the right match. I'd always envied how he could just go ahead and do things without getting stuck in indecision. He could be a little too naive sometimes, but he was pretty special. Our parents and relatives all said so—that if someone could be born with a beautiful soul, if nobility could be innate, then that was Tetsuo.

"Yayoi, pass me the tape measure?" he said.

"Here you are," I said, unearthing it from a pile of newspaper and handing it to him.

"So are you still, like, heartbroken or what? How come you're moping around at home on a Sunday?" he asked.

I'd almost forgotten, but I'd recently stopped seeing a boy, a friend of Tetsuo's, who had taken a liking to me and asked me out.

"No way. I'm just having a lazy day. I've forgotten all about him," I said, holding the end of the tape measure down for him.

"Huh," Tetsuo said, marking the plank with a felt-tip pen. "Well, you can't help it if he's leaving, I guess. It's too far."

"Definitely! He's moving to Kyushu," I said. I hadn't told Tetsuo the details, but I'd only gone out with his friend a couple of times, and it wasn't like we'd been together, or like I'd been really into him, so I wasn't that upset. But because he was the one who'd introduced us, Tetsuo felt bad that it hadn't worked out, and there in the afternoon sunlight, hearing his care for me, I suddenly felt very happy. It was a funny kind of happiness, a little sly, and maybe the sweeter for it. I didn't want to say anything so he'd never stop trying to make me feel better.

"You're really good at this kind of thing, Tetsuo."

"What thing?"

"Building a doghouse? I could never draw up a whole plan like that. Wouldn't even know where to start."

"It turns out I have a reason to do it now we have a puppy coming, you know? Wouldn't dream of doing all this work otherwise," he said, pointing at the wood he'd cut.

"True," I said.

He took up the saw again, and our conversation faded into the noise of it. I got up, slipped my sandals on, and went into the garden.

"Yayoi, would you give me a hand?" Mom said as soon as she saw me. The neatly trimmed lawn was soaking up the sun that poured down on it. She was digging a hole in the ground for a shrub that had been growing in a large pot.

"Okay, okay," I said, going over to her.

She wiped the sweat from her forehead and said, "He says he needs space for the kennel, so I'm rearranging the whole garden." She laughed.

"Now that the house is different, the garden looks new, too," I said.

The clear sunlight, not too strong, illuminated the freshly painted cream-colored walls of our new house. The plants in the garden also seemed to magically come alive as Mom gave them their new places, dirt streaking her hands and her face, her pale cheeks shining as she carefully brushed the soil from the roots of the bush she had taken out of its pot. I pulled some weeds while watching Tetsuo building the house for our new puppy beyond the glass. *He's taking it so seriously*, I thought.

"He's been working on it since seven o'clock," Mom said, noticing me watching.

"The dog isn't even here yet," I laughed.

"That would be a little too late to start," she said, and laughed, too.

Tetsuo went on sawing and hammering, unaware that he was being observed. Without the noise to bother us, the scene looked almost like a painting, and Mom and I stood still for a while on the fresh-smelling lawn, just watching.

"What an odd day it is. It can't decide if it wants to be cloudy or clear," Mom said, looking up at the sky.

The sky that afternoon was indeed a strange color. It was blanketed with layers of bright, shining clouds, and at moments the golden light pouring down from it would suddenly fade, shadowing the grass into a dull green.

"Rainy season, I guess," I said, going back to weeding. An infinite number of weeds had appeared in the garden while we'd temporarily lived in the other house, and, being only human, I'd gotten totally absorbed in the simple repetition of the task. After a while, stray drops of rain started landing where I was working, though the air was still bright.

"Well, what do you know? Dad didn't take an umbrella—I hope he isn't getting rained on."

Mom stood up where she was still transplanting several feet away. The large drops of rain falling through the sunlight gave an extra cast of concern to her expression.

"It'll stop in a minute," I said.

"Come here and get out of the rain," she said, waving me

over to where she was crouching under the low branches of a tree. "You don't want to get wet."

Sure enough, the rain was getting stronger, and a dull, dark grayness was swiftly taking over the sky. I ran over to her. We squatted together beneath the green leaves, hiding from the downpour that was now coloring in the ground around us. Inside the house, Tetsuo looked up at the sky in surprise, then waved in our direction.

"Ugh, my hair's all wet," I said.

"Yayoi." She said my name firmly, still looking out at the garden. "There's something I've been meaning to ask you . . ."

I turned to look at her, wondering what it could be.

She met my gaze with a slight hesitation in her eyes. It was the look she had when she was worrying about something she wasn't sharing. She'd called my name with the same expression on her face when Tetsuo got his first girlfriend, when I got my first period, when Dad had a breakdown from working too hard. Each time, I'd felt strangely exposed, like I had nowhere to hide. Waiting to find out what she was about to say, I felt like I was disappearing into the silent background of our family's history.

"Yayoi, was there anything unusual while we were at the other house?" Mom asked.

"The other house? You mean the place we were renting up until last week? Nope. Nothing," I said, flustered.

"I don't think so. You seemed off and down the whole time, and you still aren't yourself, even now we're back. And that night . . . I heard you shouting in the bathroom."

"Oh, that was just, a slug floating in the tub, and . . ." I tried to downplay it, but my explanation trailed off.

"Don't lie. When were you ever afraid of a slug? You've been different ever since that night. Tell me what happened," she said firmly.

The clouds filled the sky now, sending rain down from a strange mottled patchwork of light and gray. Under it, the lawn was gradually turning a deep green.

"Well, actually, I—" I said, deciding to go for it. "I saw a ghost."

"A ghost?" Mom gave me a strange look.

"Or something like that," I said.

. . . While our house was being renovated, the four of us had lived in a run-down place that was about to be pulled down on a street near the station in the next town over. My parents had started talking in the spring about how the leaky roof over Tetsuo's room would be a problem while he was studying for his exams, so the original plan had been to fix the roof, but soon enough it had escalated into a full remodel, and by the time we started looking for a temporary home, that had been the only property available. *It's only for a couple of months*, we said, and moved in immediately.

Even taking that into account, the house was quite something. It was a single-story house with just three rooms and a kitchen, and the bathroom right in the middle. Presumably, the rooms behind it had been added later, but it was an odd layout. From the rooms in the back, you had to go through the bathroom to get anywhere. The bathroom itself was a relic, its tiles all faded and chipped. It was drafty, and, worst of all, the tub leaked. The water level fell steadily so that unless the four of us bathed one right after the other, the tub would be empty by the time it was the last person's turn. All in all, though, living with inconveniences like these made an interesting change, and our stay was shaping up to be a fun bonding experience we were going through together as a family.

*

That evening, I was soaking in the aforementioned leaky tub. It was a cool night in May.

I think it was just past nine o'clock. Night air was coming in through the window that I'd opened a crack. I was quietly sitting in the tub, thinking about nothing. Somewhere by my ear I could hear a clear trickling sound almost befitting a beautiful garden fountain. But it was only the sound of the hot water gradually escaping through the cracks in the tile. Even that sound was relaxing to me now that I was used to it.

The bathroom also seemed to have a drafty gap hidden somewhere in its walls, because we found too many ants and snails and other things crawling around or cooking in the bathwater. At first I was so disgusted I really could have screamed, but I got used to them, too.

I was gazing at the dull, discolored tile mosaic under the bare light bulb. There in the steam, I suddenly felt like I might be on the verge of remembering.

That feeling—I think it's one everyone knows. It goes something like this.

A sudden rustling in your chest. A premonition of understanding. You feel you might be on the verge of uncovering something . . . You're a little fearful, oddly excited, and some-how forlorn . . . Like there's something coming around the next corner that's going to turn everything you know about yourself on its head.

But why did this feeling always make me think I was going to discover something about my past? Did other people also feel like they might be able to recall something they'd forgot-ten? I was soaking in the tub, pondering this question, when I felt something tap me on the back. Something firm floating in the water—something big.

What?

I looked behind me, startled, but there was nothing there. Just ripples in the clear water. And, when I listened, the same quiet trickling sound.

What was that . . . ? I thought, and when I turned back around, I was suddenly in a terrible mood. My body wanted to get out of there immediately, and my hair stood on end, break-ing my skin out in goose bumps even though the water was hot. I was cornered and vulnerable, and my lizard brain was sound-ing a deep and terrified warning.

Just as I tried to get to my feet, I felt something bump up against my tensed back again. Slowly, I turned my head again, and this time, it was still there.

It was a rubber duck.

A toy duck made of rubbery red plastic with its beak painted on in yellow, the kind you play with in the bath, or in a paddling pool.

I doubted my own eyes. I was baffled that something could

suddenly materialize that wasn't there before, and the more I thought about it, the more spooked I started to feel, until I shrieked loudly, stood up with a surge of water, and rushed out of the tub. Everything moved at a strange speed, like I'd just been freed from a paralytic sleep.

Mom heard me and came rushing in from the kitchen, opening the door shouting, "What happened?"

I took a breath, looked into the bath again, and—

There was nothing there.

Just the tub with quiet waves rolling across its surface, and the murmur of the water slowly draining away.

"It's nothing," I said, and went to my room and went straight to bed. My heart was still beating wildly in my chest.

When I eventually reached fitful sleep, I had a bizarre dream that didn't feel at all like a dream.

In it, I was someone else, killing a baby. Yes—the unpleasant sensation still comes back to me easily. Although it was only a flash, it had the whiff of truth.

I was standing in the bathroom, but it was full of the hot, bright sun of noon at the height of summer. The windowpanes and the tiles looked newer than I'd ever seen them. I was wearing slippers on my feet that I didn't recognize at all. They had a garish plaid pattern, and the way their soles flapped under my feet on the wooden duckboard was spine-chillingly realistic. Cold sweat trickled down my neck, and my hair was in a short style I'd never worn. I watched helplessly as, with my own hands, I held a crying baby under the cold water that filled the tub.

I'll never be able to forget the baby's weight, its futile resistance as its eyes looked into mine. My mouth was dry, and I felt dizzy. The sun was dazzling. The sound of water echoed off the walls. And there it was, in the small basin by my feet, glinting tackily in the sunlight—the toy duck . . .

Then I woke up.

＊

—I opened up to Mom for the first time about everything that had happened that day. I hadn't breathed a word about it to anyone. The sun shower continued, making my vision flicker each time I looked up to the sky. Even as I told her the story, I felt like I was glossing over things. It didn't seem real, and I just wanted to forget all about it.

"But you're sure it wasn't just a dream? You think it was real?" Mom said. She wasn't laughing. She'd always taken us seriously, even when we were kids.

"I did some research," I said. I sounded so calm I was almost scaring myself. "I talked to our landlord. Then I found a newspaper article at the library. It was the same house, and the details matched: a barmaid went out of her mind after her husband abandoned her, and killed her baby. It happened in summer, just like in my dream. August."

". . . I see," Mom said, sinking into thought.

"Mom, when I was younger—did I ever see things?" I asked.

"Why?" she said quickly.

I turned to her, and my heart ached to see the clouds in her eyes.

"It's just a feeling I get."

It was a topic I should let lie, I knew. It was like teetering across a tightrope on a lonely night, when all you can see in the dark is your own feet on the white rope. You don't feel ready, but there's no going back. I kept staring at the grass.

"You were a terribly sensitive child. I read books about it. Precognition, ESP, you know. Dad doesn't believe in any of that, so he wasn't too concerned. But when you were really small, you used to tell us who was calling every time the phone rang. Even the people you didn't know—you'd say, *Someone called Yamamoto*, or, *It's a person from Daddy's work*. And you were almost always right. You'd also sense things that had happened in the past. The one I always think of is when we went to Shichirigahama. You said, *There was a big battle here a long, long time ago*. That gave me a fright. And you'd stay away from accident sites, and railway crossings where people had been killed, even though we never told you about them. Isn't that amazing? You probably don't remember . . . Oh, and when Dad and I had a blow-up? We'd do it after you and Tetsuo went to bed, so you'd be all smiles at breakfast, but the moment you went into our room you'd say, *Mommy, Daddy, are you fighting?* It happened so much we took you around several different clinics to get specialist opinions, but in the end, it kind of stopped as you got older."

"I didn't know that." None of this even rang a bell.

"It's true. I remember thinking how hard it seemed to be for you. To be able to see, at a glance, what other people don't—but maybe that's not so bad while you're young. Children are like that anyway, to a greater or lesser extent, aren't they? But as much as it was a gift, Dad and I, we didn't want you to end up like—you know, those people you see on TV, that psychic Monsieur Croiset, or the spoon-bending boy. We wanted you to have a normal, easy life. We were worried that if that ability was going to stick around once your spirit no longer had the freedom of being a kid, if it kept expressing itself against your will once you were an adult—then you'd either need to spend an awful lot of energy trying to control it, or end up in an institution, one way or another. Do you know what I'm saying? We talked about it a lot because we were worried for you. A long time ago now."

"I get it," I said. "But that was then. It's not what I'm worried about. My question is, why did I see what I saw when we were in the other house? I'm not sure, but if it was just triggered by the leftover thoughts lingering at the scene of a crime, then it won't happen again."

"I hadn't thought of it that way," she said, finally smiling in relief. "Then we have nothing to worry about. Let's put it behind us and enjoy our new house."

"Let's do that."

I agreed wholeheartedly, but I felt dismayed by how much of myself I hadn't been aware of. There was too much I didn't remember. Too many parts that were hidden away from myself. The rain stopped, and immediately, the sun came out and lit up the entire garden like the rain had never been. We resumed our gardening.

Looking back, it's obvious the afternoon of the sun shower

was a major turning point. That day, that Sunday, my family was all there at home, doing our own things. It was a gentle, ordinary day.

But a huge tide was already incoming. As much as I cherished its peacefulness, a handful of images crossed my vision that day that I was unable to deny. I could only watch in astonishment while they unspooled in a stream like an old 8 mm film clattering into motion, distant and yet treasured, filling my heart up with pain and longing.

The first was a hand. An old woman's hand holding a pair of shears, putting some flowers in a vase. The hand wasn't my mom's. It was wearing an emerald ring. It was a slender, woman's hand.

Another was the image of a happy couple, walking slowly, seen from behind. The woman had to be the one whose hand I'd just seen.

These visions continued to flow in a place wholly set apart from the real world around me. I held my breath, to try to retain as much of them as I could as they appeared and then disappeared in succession. They seemed to sear my eyes and pass too quickly, as if I were watching my favorite landscapes on earth through the window of a speeding car. The longest and most memorable was the scene with the girl who was my sister.

She was young, and had her hair in tails. She was looking up at a window with an oddly mature expression. She stood near the edge of a deep green lake, wearing red sandals that looked bright against the gray of the flagstones, and called out my name with a pensive look.

"Yayoi."

Her voice was sweet. The lukewarm breeze brushed past her hair. Her familiar profile looked up warily at the overcast sky. I stood with her, watching the clouds in the far distance streaming past, blown by the wind.

"Yayoi, there's a typhoon coming."

In that moment, I had no doubt this girl was my older sister. I didn't say anything, but nodded. She turned to me and smiled.

"We'll lay our mattresses by the window tonight and watch the storm."

*

A few days later, night. I was on my balcony, very slowly sipping a good well-chilled sake. It was a brief interlude in the rainy season, and the stars were out.

Although it was small, my new room had a balcony, which I was very satisfied with. I loved being in the open air, no matter the season.

But the balcony was so narrow there was barely room for me to sit down. I was leaning heavily against the concrete wall with both feet up on the air-con unit, wedged uncomfortably between the sliding glass door I'd closed firmly behind me and the tall railing, looking up at the starry sky beyond. The brisk breeze felt good on my cheeks. I submerged myself in the sweet June chill all the way to the tips of my fingernails. The air I was breathing was so clear I thought I might drift off to sleep. Every last star was blinking.

I was in two minds.

I'd always had a habit of running away from home. Whenever I had some deep thinking to do, I felt the need to get away. It was restorative just being in a place where there were no family dinners, no *How did you sleep*, no Mom or Dad or Tetsuo.

But I knew this was only a kind of make-believe. When I

came back home after taking some time out to change my perspective, I could always count on my parents welcoming me back with a smile once they were done huffing and pouting. *I guess you need to have a home before you can run away from it,* I thought, and I felt it in my heart.

But something felt different this time. I kept second-guessing myself. I started packing my travel duffel, and stopped again. *There's no coming back to what I have now, not this time. Leaving now means setting something big into motion.*

Somehow, I was sure of it.

This was home. When I came back after a few days away like I always did, things would be the same on the surface. But still, I knew. Every time I thought about leaving, the memory of Dad's broad shoulders or Mom's smile seemed to pierce my chest and make it ache, and I'd sink into thought before my half-packed duffel.

It was even harder with Tetsuo.

Every time I saw him, his eager eyes and innocent demeanor, I know I didn't want to lose or miss out on a single piece of what we had.

Just then, through the glass, I heard a knock at the door of my room. I floundered, trying to get up, but between the constricted space and feeling a little drunk, I gave up and shouted, "Come in!"

There was something odd about calling someone into a room that I wasn't actually in myself, and I watched Tetsuo open the door and stride in to a room that felt as distant as something in a movie. He came straight over to the window.

"What are you doing? You look like a giant salamander that decided to flip upside down and lie there until it got too fat for its tank," I heard him say through the glass door.

He was standing in my room barefoot, wearing jeans and a heather-gray T-shirt. As usual, he had a workbook in one hand, and he looked at me with his spine straight and eyes that seemed dangerous in their clarity.

. . . I have family, blood family, somewhere . . . not here.

It was impossible to believe. How could it possibly be true? But it was no more unlikely than me remembering nothing of my childhood. And more convincingly, something deep in my heart shone its light of truth. This kind of knowing was never wrong . . . even when I wished it could be.

All this made me feel unmoored, like I was up in the air.

I wanted Tetsuo to save me. To tell me, in his frank, confident way, "It doesn't matter. Just forget about it." *If only I could forget and feel free*, I thought. But I didn't tell him any of that. Instead, I slid open the door to my room. *It's this glass coming between us in the dark making things feel so raw. Get rid of it.*

"What?" I said to him, without getting up.

"Nothing, I just needed some packaging tape. Didn't you have it in here?" he said.

"It's on my desk."

"Why are you sitting like that?"

"I felt like being outside."

"You're happy with your new balcony," he said, and laughed merrily.

His voice carried through the darkness and seemed to light

a shining path through the night sky. Just his tone was enough to reassure me. *It's because he loves me*, I thought. *And I love him, too. Simple.*

But instead of all the different things I wanted to say, I said, a little tipsily, "Don't you think nights are so pretty, Tetsuo?"

And instead of rolling his eyes, he said, "It's because the air's always clearer at night." Then he took the roll of tape and left the room.

His words slowly settled into my heart, leaving a sweet resonance behind them.

Tetsuo often went out in the evenings.

People would call the house and tell him what was happening that night. Sometimes it was a girl, and sometimes one of his male friends. He knew a lot of people. When he went out, the whole house suddenly felt empty. It was the loneliness of having a corner of your heart that was waiting for someone. Without the small pieces of his presence in the house—his long limbs, his footfalls, his back when I passed behind him—I was bored. I could be talking on the phone, laughing, or watching TV, but my attention was still on the front door. Especially on days when I was feeling down, and lying in bed trying to sleep at night, the sound of Tetsuo opening the front door and coming upstairs made me feel safe. I wouldn't go out to greet him or anything. But the sounds of him in the house would reassure me like a lullaby until I fell asleep.

I'd never figured out why I got so lonely so easily. Sometimes when I was on my own at night, I'd be seized by an overwhelming sadness I could only call homesickness. Tetsuo was the only one I could count on to fill that hole for me. When he was around I never felt in danger, no matter how despondent I got. But each time I reached the verge of remembering something, I felt vulnerable. Like a traveler far from home, I lost touch with the security of feeling that I could stay right where I was.

The call that came in for Tetsuo that night was a bad one. When I picked up, there was a man's voice I didn't recognize on the other end of the line. *Another late-night meeting*, I thought. His school was known in the area for having more than its share of fights and bullies.

As his sister, though, it wasn't my place to say anything. Tetsuo was in his room, so I yelled, "It's for you!" I watched his door open. It took only a moment for him to make his way downstairs, his feet hitting each step rhythmically, but in those few seconds I looked into his innocent eyes and didn't want him to go. I hadn't felt anything like that until I saw him. I didn't want to hand over the phone and watch his happy eyes cloud over. The wish was so strong it that was almost blinding, and for a split second I felt like I might fall to pieces.

I passed him the receiver without saying anything, then climbed up the stairs and retreated to my room. After a while, I heard Tetsuo shut the front door behind him.

Everything was normal, except the way I felt in my heart.

Up until then, my concern when Tetsuo stayed out all night or hurt himself was only cursory. That night, for the first time, in the transparent dark of early summer, I felt sick to my stomach with worry for him. There was something different in the shape of the moon I saw through the window, the smell of the night, and most of all, what passed between us as I handed him the phone and he looked into my eyes. It had happened in an instant, but left a strangely visceral imprint within my chest.

I was in my room, waiting for Tetsuo to come home. Somewhere deep in my ears I registered the ticking of the clock coldly marking time. At some point, I abandoned the comics I'd been reading to pretend there was nothing going on and the homework I'd started to fill the time, and went and stood by the window, looking down into the darkness, just waiting for him to come through the gate.

I still can't explain how it happened.

I didn't know where he'd gone that night. There were three roads he could have taken that led back to the house. Before I could think about it, I was dressed and going out the front door as if that had been the plan all along. The night air blew through the town as if it were immaterial, and in the distance I heard the roar of high winds. The silhouetted trees in the garden lurched and rustled, and behind them I could see the light still on in my parents' window. It didn't matter. I stepped out onto the dark street in search of Tetsuo. I turned down countless side streets, and as my breath got shorter, my rational questions—*What am I doing? Why does my brother need me to run through the night looking for him?*—leached out into the darkness surrounding me, leaving behind only a frantic longing, like that of a lost child. *It's almost like I'm in love*, I thought, as I canvassed the blocks of our neighborhood.

But that romance came to an end the second I found him, on a corner a considerable distance from home.

"Hey, Tetsuo," I heard myself say in a calm, sisterly voice.

"What, are you—out on a walk?" Tetsuo looked taken by surprise. He didn't have any obvious injuries, which was a relief.

Smiling, I said, "You were in a fight."

"How did you know?" he said, smiling too. "It was a dumb argument. No big deal."

"Geniuses are always misunderstood," I said. We started walking home, side by side.

"I'm hungry. Can we go get something to eat? I want to get rid of this bad taste in my mouth," Tetsuo said.

"Where was it?"

"The shrine. It wasn't even a fight. There were some so-called upperclassmen trying to throw their weight around, but they were full of shit, so I shoved them out of the way and left. That's all."

"Sure."

This felt new. I didn't really know how things had been for Tetsuo at school since he started high school. As we talked, we walked slowly, peacefully, as though we were making our way across the seabed of night.

We stopped at the McDonald's by the station, but I realized I didn't have my wallet, so Tetsuo paid for both of us. We ordered everything we wanted, and ate until we were full. I felt strangely elated. I wanted to stay out with Tetsuo forever.

As we left the restaurant, he laughed and said, "I can't

believe you made me treat you after the night I've had. Talk about kicking me when I'm down."

"I'll pay you back as soon as we get home," I said, laughing too.

"That hit the spot, though. I've forgotten all about those idiots," he said, looking up at the sky.

"Good for you," I said. It felt very sweet to be going home with him. My vision was so clear I felt I could reach out and touch the wind as it passed in the distance. It was late enough that there were only a few people around the station, and the occasional storefront light outlined the night like at the end of a festival.

Tetsuo and I were together in a feeling similar to what we'd experienced each time we went through something big growing up—when the trees we'd planted as a family had all been uprooted by a typhoon, or at the death of one of our relatives.

Out of nowhere, Tetsuo said, "Yayoi, isn't the night even more beautiful tonight? Like the lights and stuff. Don't you think there's something different about them?"

That was exactly what I'd been thinking while we walked. The night sky was truly black, and the open air reflected the town like a polished mirror.

"I think you're right," I remember saying. "It must be because the air's extra clear tonight."

As if by some chemical reaction, fear started rising in me as soon as Tetsuo left my room and the door closed loudly behind him. I wanted to get up from the balcony, follow him to his room, and tell him what was on my mind.

But I didn't.

I stayed there, looking into the night sky.

The next night, it rained again, and I ran away from home.

*

My aunt loved the *Friday the 13th* movies, and that night, she was lying on the floor engrossed in watching whichever installments she'd checked out from the video rental place that week.

"What do you like so much about them?" I'd asked her.

After thinking for a minute, she said, "It's nice how the same person always comes back. So you don't feel lonely."

I made some deductions. Could she be talking about . . . Jason? And was my aunt lonely?

We were full, having just finished eating a small mountain of caramel flan. Although she never cooked meals, my aunt often made flan. We ate it with soup spoons straight out of the mixing bowl. Its sweet smell permeated all the corners of the brightly lit room. I'd cooked dinner that evening, but the flan far outweighed the main dish.

My aunt was lying in her bathrobe, her hair still wet. When the gory scenes came on, she got up and crept close to the TV, and when the tension passed, she collapsed back on the floor again. From time to time, she sneezed or yawned or rubbed at her hair with a big towel. I was on the sofa, also watching the movie, but actually far more entertained by observing the contrast between the bloodcurdling screams coming from the screen and her reactions.

I'd been at my aunt's for a while now. Time had come to a complete stop, and aside from going to school, I spent almost all my time at her house. Over the days I spent with her, watching her closely, I was becoming more and more aware of how the way her eyebrows looked when her bangs were swept back, or her face in profile when she was focused on something, or something in the way she looked away from things reminded me of the girl in the visions that had come to me on the day of the sun shower.

It took me a while to admit it: *There's no point pretending—I came here because I knew. Except now that I'm here, I'm not sure what to do. So here we are.*

My aunt didn't seem to care, so neither did I. I didn't know how or why we'd been separated, but until I found out, I wanted to spend as long as I could incubating the faint echoes of memory that were coming to me, piece by piece.

The movie was still playing, but on the sofa, I was starting to nod off. Since coming here, I often ended up falling asleep like this. Every spot in the house was a potential bed, and when I fell asleep, my aunt would find me and cover me with a blanket wherever I was.

I heard the phone ring even in my sleep: it rang out like a wind chime in a distant window through my slow and muted awareness. Waking in stages, I saw from between barely open eyelids my aunt pick up the receiver and say, "Hello?"

". . . Oh, well, yeah. Mm-hmm, this whole time. It's okay. I don't mind. Okay."

The moment I understood that she was talking to Mom, I went straight back to feigning sleep. I sensed my aunt glance in my direction—then the conversation continued.

"No, I'm not trying to do that. Listen, that's not what it's about . . . I don't see why we shouldn't spend some time together. I'll send her back the minute she wants to leave. She's not a child anymore. You're worrying too much. Of course I'd never. You know that."

My aunt's evanescent murmur seemed to just barely reach my ears. There was always something melancholy about late-night phone calls. And discovering the truth always hurt. I eavesdropped from the border between dreaming and waking, feeling like a child.

Mom and Dad, who'd brought me up; the shape of Tetsuo's arms; my real parents, whom I'd recalled for just a moment. Her soft hands and their kind-looking backs. I didn't even remember their names. Everything was so far away . . . After more back-and-forth with Mom, my aunt put the receiver down with a faint ring. Then, sighing, she went back into the private world of her movie. I was strangely pleased that she'd looked out for me. That as much as she would go to great lengths to avoid getting involved in things she didn't want to deal with, she hadn't woken me up and made me talk to Mom, but instead, with sisterly care, had let me sleep.

"Yayoi, have a drink with me," my aunt was saying, shaking me awake. I opened my eyes with a start. The clock said it was 2 a.m.

I couldn't believe I'd been asleep for almost two hours. "Huh? What? Drink?" I said groggily.

My aunt looked at me a little sullen and said, "I finished the movies. I'm not sleepy at all, and I don't have school tomorrow. Let's drink."

"Okay, okay," I said, still confused, and got up to get the ice. My aunt was pulling bottles of whiskey and mineral water out of the underfloor cupboard. Even the sound of her clunking them down on the floor thrilled me. She was so much older, and when I was with her, I felt like I had nothing to fear. Not the dark of night, nor everything I still didn't know about myself. Strange to think how I'd always felt anxious in my warm home, yet here, where daily life felt so precarious, I was fulfilled. The illusion that I'd always lived like this seemed to be infiltrating my body. Could it be that it was in my blood?

The white lace curtains swayed against the frame of the open window, and the occasional leaf from the garden drifted inside. Faint sounds of cars and sirens from far away arrived, carried on the wind. Had Mom, Dad, and Tetsuo sat down to a happy evening meal tonight? And if I hadn't figured it out, then would my aunt have kept on pretending she was just my aunt for the rest of her life?

I sat in the moonlight, wondering.

*

The phone rang.

Mom again? My aunt must have thought the same. She acted as though she couldn't hear it ringing at all. She ignored it so coolly that I wondered whether I was in a dark dawn somewhere, dreaming about an alarm clock.

The phone went on ringing like it meant business—ten, twenty more rings, disturbing the air of the quiet room.

I no longer had the ability to tell who was on the other end of the line like I once did. But I could still sense something coming through. I closed my eyes and drew it toward me. I felt the shadow of a kind of passion on the other end. He was gripping the receiver with a feeling that was almost romantic. The lineaments of that love felt familiar to me, and I closed my eyes and carefully retraced them. A little brusque, but honest, and loyal . . .

"Oh, be quiet," my aunt said, giving in and picking up the phone. Assuming it must be her boyfriend, I tried to retreat discreetly into the kitchen.

"Yayoi," I heard her say. She was holding out the receiver. "It's for you."

I went to her and took it gingerly. "Hello?" I said.

"Hello?" I heard Tetsuo say, and I knew he'd picked up on something. The Tetsuo his voice conjured up was the young boy who had wanted to sleep next to me on nights we'd heard a scary story.

"Tetsuo? It's late. What's up?"

"I was waiting for Mom and Dad to go to bed . . . Yayoi, are you good?"

"Yeah."

"How come you're at Aunt Yukino's? Something happen?"

"Not really . . . Have you been studying?"

"Sure, every day. It's no fun having a new house without you."

He'd always been the kind of kid who didn't hesitate to say how he was feeling—if he liked something or disliked it, if he was hot or cold, sleepy or hungry. When I seemed down, he didn't hold back from trying to cheer me up.

"Thanks. But it's nothing major. I'll come home soon."

He was also quick to pick up on lies like this one.

"You sure? Well, I'm here for you."

That call felt charmed, as if Tetsuo was intuiting everything that was hidden behind my words. I found it hard to believe that until very recently I'd shared a house like it was no big deal with the same voice that was now coming to me across the night.

At Tetsuo's trying to console me, I smiled inwardly and said, "I told you, I'm fine." As his older sibling, I sometimes defaulted to being combative for no real reason.

But he let me have my moment of petty bluster, and said kindly, "All right. See you soon," before hanging up.

I put the receiver back softly, and didn't say anything.

My aunt had been watching me the whole time. After a short silence, she said, "He wants you back?"

". . . Yeah," I said, nodding.

"Hm."

She looked a little sad.

I wanted to see Tetsuo. I was enjoying my life here; at the same time, I thought of him each time I gazed into the trees, or walked through the smell of back streets in the rainy season, or looked up at a gray sky. My thoughts always ended up at the same place. *If we're not brother and sister . . . then . . .* But I loved our parents and didn't want to hurt them, and there wasn't enough space, and it wasn't right somehow—and there my thoughts would stop, slowly melting away into the atmosphere in this house, which was nothing but gentle.

"Let's get started," my aunt said.

We didn't have any savory snacks to go with our whiskey, so we decided to have the rest of the flan and some black cherries that were in the refrigerator. It was a slightly nauseating combination.

I'd never had the chance to drink with my aunt before.

I'd suspected she might be the type of drinker who went all out once she got started, and I was right.

"Do you usually drink this much even when you're alone?" I asked.

"Yep," she said.

She poured another good measure of whiskey over the ice filling her glass. I'd been watching the shadow it cast on the floor each time it slowly filled up, accompanied by the clink of ice cubes settling. As I looked, it gradually dawned on me— *She isn't invulnerable, either. Her life in this house isn't always fun and games. And I've disrupted something by coming here.*

"He likes you, huh?" she said, smiling slightly. She was studying the shape of her toenails at the ends of her outstretched legs.

"You mean Tetsuo?" I said.

"Yeah, your nonbiological brother," she said carelessly.

There were no secrets left. In that moment, everything— the glow of the lamp, the color of the sky outside the window, and each passing drop of precious time—seemed to take on a new light.

Now, I thought. *This is my chance.*

Calmly, I asked, "What were our parents like?"

She answered easily, as if she'd never been hiding anything.

"They were kind people," she said quietly, lowering her lashes. "We lived in a house with a pond in the garden."

"Yes. Were we happy?"

"Indescribably so," she said.

She went on. "The people you live with now are good people, in their own way. But we had something different. Like a fairy tale—so happy you maybe knew it was too good to last . . . But you were so small, Yayoi. Maybe you've forgotten, even if you knew it then."

My aunt had given up looking like my aunt and turned into my older sister. Her expression was open to me, her gaze no longer averted. She was so present that the intensity of it frightened me. *This is what she was really like*, I thought. *A woman with eyes that can see straight into your heart.*

"Do you remember me having . . . weird abilities?" I asked.

"Yes, let's see. You were an odd child, even before you learned to talk. You'd sense things that had happened in the past. And when we got phone calls from people our parents didn't like, you'd start wailing as if you were on fire. We'd laugh and wonder if you could read their minds. It was kind of fun, actually. We used to say every family ought to have one . . ."

She smiled. She seemed so matter-of-fact about it that I simply forgot the worries and cares I'd been carrying around with me. For some time after that, she gazed out the window with a faraway look, like she was reeling in the beautiful strands she would need for the old stories she was preparing to weave for me. The moon shone small and far away in the sky. It was jarring to discover that my aunt was so separate from everything already, when it had been such a major upheaval for me. For her, it was all in the past. It gave me hope that I, too, would be able to see it that way some day.

"Did you have . . . anything like that?"

"Nope," she said readily. Her slender fingers grabbed a few cherries and put them on the palm of her other hand. Popping one in her mouth, she said, "Remind me—is it bad to have fruit when you're drinking?"

"I think so. You need something with protein."

She giggled. "You sound just like your mom. I know you've had a happy life, so maybe it's too bad you have to remember the truth. You know—none of them are actually related to us at all, including your grandpa who died. They just took us in because they were so close with our real parents. They're all really good people. The boy, too."

"Tetsuo?"

"Yeah." She nodded. "Don't you think so? He understands a lot more than he thinks he knows."

"Maybe you're right," I said. That was something I couldn't think about yet. "But I . . . There's still a lot I don't remember. Why did our parents die? And why did I forget?"

My aunt frowned, looking a little pained.

"We were on a . . . our last family vacation."

She started to tell the story, and I held my breath and listened.

"We went up to Aomori. You were still really young. Our dad was driving the new car, and he understeered around a corner on a winding mountain road. It was a head-on collision. We saw everything from the back seat. Watched our mom and dad die— Well, maybe you didn't. I grabbed you and we crawled out of the car, covered in blood. Everything was wrecked. My head hurt. The leaves were turning, and there was blood in my eyes, and everything looked deep red. Then I passed out, too. See this scar?"

She pointed to a mark on her forehead by her hairline.

"Our mom and dad died instantly. The other driver was okay. Thank god. They were such gentle people, it would have killed them to know they'd hurt anyone else. They were almost too good for this world. You were in a pretty bad state of shock, and had to stay in the hospital for a long time . . . which explains why you don't remember."

My heart gave a squeeze each time I heard her say *our mom and dad*.

". . . But they took us both in," I said. "Mom, Dad, and Tetsuo. I don't understand why they made you live by yourself."

No, I couldn't picture my parents, being the people they were, not suggesting that she come and live with us, too.

"I insisted. Your mom tried to talk me into it, of course, repeatedly. No wonder. I was still in high school. I was the one who said I wanted you to be my niece. And your grandpa gave me this house."

"Why?"

"I wanted to be alone. I didn't want to deal with it. It was okay for you—you were still young enough to start over. But I couldn't forget the life we'd had with our real mom and dad. I couldn't picture myself living any other way. Not that I believe that now, but . . ."

She's a princess asleep in an old castle where time's stopped, clinging to dreams of a lost dynasty, I thought. She was the only one left who knew its glory, and her heart belonged to it. What a prideful way to live! What was this thing that held her in its ruthless clutches like a deadly disease? I was trying not to feel like she'd abandoned me. I knew it wasn't like that. But the distance it had opened up between the two of us seemed impossible to close—even more reason why here, tonight, we were in a fleeting dream, outside time and space.

"I'm sorry I didn't remember. All this time. Do you blame me? Did you miss me?" I said.

She looked at me and then gradually, just like always, gave me a muted smile. It was a perfect smile that contained everything that existed in the world, like a lake brimming with cold, clear water.

I felt forgiven.

"I hope you remember more about them soon," she said. "We were an unusual family, maybe, but we were happy. As happy as a dream.

"Dad was a scholar, a total eccentric. So there was no such thing as a normal day in our home. Sometimes we'd all dress up and go out to dinner on a whim, but if it rained for a week, Mom would refuse to go out shopping and we'd have a single piece of bread to share between us. When the snow was heavy, or on nights when it stormed, the four of us would huddle close by the window and go to sleep watching the sky . . . We traveled all over, too. We'd leave without making a plan, and camp. We lived in the mountains for a month once. I remember playing cards and making you guess the suit. You always liked it when we said you were right. Even though you were so young. Yes, it was a little like living in Moomin Valley, where the sun never sets. Days that were endless, but which you could only take one at a time, with no sense of what was coming tomorrow . . . I still can't shake it. It lives inside me like a curse or a blessing."

As she spoke, I tried to project my mind toward the vision

of our family her eyes could see. Even though I couldn't remember any of it, my heart ached all the same.

Maybe I was jealous of her for having those memories.

I went to bed drunk, so my sleep was unusually shallow and
dreamless. But liberated from the anxiety of not knowing, it
was suffused with a soft light. For the first time in a while I
had the sensation of being gently comforted, as if I were sitting
in a patch of sunlight and watching the sun drift between distant clouds. I hadn't been sleeping well at all. Then, as I dozed,
I heard the sound of the piano. It rang out so beautifully that I
found myself crying hot tears. Its melody filled up my dream,
over and over, before disappearing with a sparkle somewhere
deep inside my chest.

*

I know I heard the sound of the front door closing behind my aunt when she left. I glanced out the window, where the night was starting to give way to dawn. Her footsteps rang out under a strange pink sky. I could hear it all clearly because the upstairs room I was sleeping in was directly above the entrance hall. I remember her fading footsteps quite clearly.

Drowsily, I wondered, *Where's she going?* before falling back into a deeper sleep.

When I next woke, it was just past ten o'clock. I felt too groggy to get up, so I lay there in silence, gazing out of the window. Bright, wispy clouds lay over the clear sky, and the vaguely refreshing scent of trees arrived on the wind from somewhere far away. Called back into a breezy sleep, I slowly closed my eyes again. I felt the light peeping gently on my eyelids.

The doorbell rang.

Thinking I would just ignore it if it was a salesperson or a bill collector, I snuck a look out the window, down at the front door. I could see someone's head between the lush green leaves. In astonishment, I recognized the shape of those shoulders under that collared shirt, and the whorl in the hair.

"Tetsuo!" I called down to him.

My dear brother's face slowly turned up toward mine. Our gazes met, and he seemed like someone I hadn't seen in a very long time—even though it had only been a week.

"Were you in bed? You're living the life of Riley," Tetsuo said, and laughed. Buried among the plants, he looked up at me, seeming well. My heart was suddenly drawn to him. All the noise around me quieted, and even the light and wind seemed to take a step back.

"Why are you here? Come on up," I said, smiling at him.

"Where's Aunt Yukino?"

"I think she went out."

"I can't, I'm on my way to school. Just thought I'd drop by."

". . . Oh. Too bad."

"Want me to come back when I'm done?"

"Of course," I said, and smiled again. It felt like a happy, natural smile that could have made a flower bloom.

Tetsuo's eyes softened in relief.

"Then I'll see you later," he said, and went back down the path, through the gate, and on his way. I thought about the way he stood tall, and his tatty schoolbag, the bright and airy house he'd just come from. I noticed that the affection I felt for him now had the same quality as the affection I had for the past. And we were different now. We were boy and girl, two strangers harboring budding feelings for each other.

Maybe it's about time I went home, I thought—calmly, hopefully.

Later, when Tetsuo came back, I'd make him carry my duffel, and we'd go back home to our parents. I'd live quietly for a while, not letting on what I knew, and come back to visit my aunt from time to time.

As soon as I made the decision, my appetite reared its head, so I went down to the kitchen to find something to eat. The whole house fell silent like a cemetery as soon as my aunt left. The furniture and knickknacks, even the magazines left open in random places—everything seemed to be in its right place, holding its breath, waiting. Last night's dishes were soaking in the sink. I washed up, even the splashing of water sounding loud in the stillness. The cold water felt good on my hands. Pure, white light streamed in through the window and lit up a section of the floor. I sat down at the table, where the sun was as steady as if this were the seaside at high summer, and ate some bread, drank some orange juice, and picked at the rest of the black cherries. It was so bright I felt as if I were having a picnic. The cool floor felt rough underfoot. Outside the window, the world was divided neatly into light and shadow, and the pre-summer filigree formed by the tree branches flickered in the breeze. The sun was growing stronger toward afternoon. I sat there drinking in my fill of the signs of summer just coming around the corner.

It was only later in the afternoon that I noticed something seemed off.

My aunt wasn't back. Belatedly, I realized I knew nothing about her personal life. Was she seeing anyone? Did she have friends she might have gone to stay with? What neighborhood did she go shopping in? I had no clue about any of it. My aunt's life was devoid of the echoes these details would normally have left.

The biggest thing, though, was that the house seemed different. While normally, time seemed to lie thick within its walls, it now felt completely vacant. Looking around the dusty house, I even wondered if it had all been a dream.

I went to my aunt's room and opened the door.

It was as much of a mess as ever. All her things were out, drawers hung open, and clothes were strewn everywhere, like a burglar had just gone through everything. Her desk was also a mess, covered in objects that might have been the contents of an upended handbag. A layer of dust lay on the windowsills, and the mirror on the wall was cloudy, like some ancient artifact that had only recently been unearthed. *It's practically magic the way she looks so prim and proper when she goes to work. How does she do it?* I wondered as I stepped back out of the room. As soon as I shut the door behind me, I thought, based on nothing in particular: *She isn't going to be back anytime soon.*

*

"Nothing good ever comes of leaving suddenly," Mom, who used to be a nurse, would often say.

"I can't tell you how many times I've seen family members who've been caring for a patient step away for just a minute and miss their loved one's last breath."

That's just how chance works, she'd say. Had she recognized the shadow of my aunt in me then, the way I'd go out and stay out when the mood took me, without a word to let them know? Did she see habits that were in my blood, irrepressible by the mere passage of time?

"What if Dad or I had an accident and got taken to hospital, or, god forbid, passed away, Yayoi? And we didn't know how to reach you?"

She said it in all seriousness, and I loved that about her, and the way she saw things.

"You'd have to live with the weight of that phone call forever. For the rest of your life."

Not me, I thought. *It wouldn't bother me like that. That's the kind of daughter I am.* And the feeling wasn't just in protest of being scolded for staying out all night. I knew it with a cold certainty that went deep down.

I remember deciding not to tell her that, though, because I thought it would hurt her if I did.

*

By early evening, as I'd predicted, my aunt still wasn't back.

I was sitting at the kitchen table in the gloom. I hadn't switched on any lights. I didn't know what to do. The world outside the window seemed to be floating in bluish light that turned the trees into layered black paper cutouts. I could have watched their rustling outlines endlessly. I was thinking, vaguely, about my aunt living for so long here on her own.

It didn't seem to have been too hard of a life.

But how badly had I complicated things for her by coming here?

The doubt drove me several times to her room, where I searched the clutter on her desk for clues, but each time, I came back down to the kitchen after finding nothing—no note, or anything to indicate where she'd gone.

The doorbell rang.

"I'm coming in," Tetsuo said, coming inside.

He found me sitting at the table in the dark. Startled, he said, "What's going on? Why are you sitting in the dark like you're an axe murderer?"

"I'm not," I said. "She left. I don't know where she is."

As soon as I spoke to Tetsuo, the feelings I couldn't feel

clearly when I was trying to think them through on my own came rushing to the surface. I was worried, and anxious.

"Let's get some lights on in here," Tetsuo said, feeling around for the switch on the wall. He found it, and instantly the world outside sank back into deep shadow. *We're back in night again*, I thought. I couldn't seem to gather my thoughts.

Tetsuo was still in his school uniform. Putting his bag on the table, he sat down heavily opposite me. His movements were always deliberate and precise—or maybe they just looked that way to me. I'd always admired the steadiness of his gaze. Compared to him, I felt like I was just sitting on the sidelines, indecisive, watching things pass me by.

"Was there some reason she had to leave?" he said.

"I think there might have been."

"So she's disappeared off somewhere, like what happened at the funeral," he said. "You don't know where?"

"I really don't. She didn't say a word to me. For all I know, she might even be back soon. But I have this hunch she's gone somewhere really far away."

". . . A hunch, huh? I'm sure you're right, yours are usually pretty good. And I'm going to guess—she probably wants you to go find her."

"What do you mean?" I said, surprised.

"I mean, she knows you're here. Isn't it obvious? When people like her get it into their heads to do something selfish for once, they can get a little carried away. Either that, or she wants you to stay here and wait for her. She's saying, *Don't leave me. What do you think?"*

"Oh, I get it. That didn't occur to me. But you could be right."

Seen through Tetsuo's eyes, my aunt seemed a little more fragile, a little more real. I stood up without a word and decided to make some tea. In contrast to her usual slapdash style, my aunt stored her different varieties of tea in neat glass jars. It pained me to see it. This must have been how all the tea was kept in the home we had once lived in together so long ago. Each jar was labeled in her winsome handwriting. I warmed two cups, measured out the tea leaves for the pot, and brewed the tea with far more care than usual.

The desire to share everything I'd discovered with Tetsuo and involve him in the whole affair was whirling around my mind, almost unstoppably. It was to try to quiet it that I made the tea so carefully.

I didn't want to do something I'd forever regret.

Silently, I handed him the tea.

"Where's the sugar?" he asked.

"Beats me," I said.

"What a way to live," he said, sipping his tea. He looked around the room. "This house feels like it's been empty for years."

At his words, I was suddenly seized by a heartbreaking fantasy: What if I'd never even had an aunt? Everyone else had died in the accident, and I was the only one who'd ever set foot in this house, while the rest of my family watched over me from somewhere else. The night I'd turned up with an overstuffed duffel, it had been my sister's ghost who had taken pity on me and welcomed me in. All my family were friendly ghosts.

"I think I've got it," Tetsuo said.

While I'd been indulging in a dead-end reverie that was harmless, but also not helpful either, he'd been putting his mind to use.

"That cabin our relatives own. You know, near the big Seibu," he said.

"The what?"

"There's a Seibu department store in the mountains, except it's only one story high, like a farmer's market or something . . . Where was that?"

"Oh, you mean Karuizawa?" I said.

"That's it. I know she likes it there, and uses the cabin a lot. It's not that far. Close enough you could decide to go on a whim."

"You could be right," I said.

I suddenly felt like there was hope. I was sure she was there, I could sense it. The cabin in the woods, where I'd been a few times when we were younger, too. *I need to go there*, I decided. But was it really the single-story Seibu store that Tetsuo remembered it by, and not the late-afternoon sun angling through the trees, or the cool breezes that blew over the mountain meadows? Sure, he would only have been a boy then. *But what a strange child*, I thought, looking at him.

He looked straight back at me, and said, "Are you going?"

"Yeah, I'll go check. It'll take me another couple of days, but could you come up with an excuse for Mom and Dad? You can't tell them she's gone," I said.

"I'm coming with you," he said immediately.

He sounded so matter-of-fact that for a second I was lost for words.

"You can't," I said.

"Why not?" he said. He gazed at me steadily, his eyes containing just the appearance of romantic intent, and I didn't know what to do.

"You can't just up and leave! What will you say to Mom and Dad? You'll need your toothbrush, and clean underwear, and stuff."

"Let me tell you something," Tetsuo said with a sigh. "Unlike you, I'm not scared of making a move. I do this kind of thing all the time. You can buy that stuff in any store, and coming up with an excuse is like picking out a star in the sky. There's no reason for anyone to suspect what I'm doing has anything to do with you or Aunt Yukino."

I stayed silent for a minute. Then I thought, *Screw it. Who cares what happens? At least it'll be an adventure.*

"Then will you come with me, Tetsuo?"

"Sure thing. Let's get moving. I don't think she's the type to kill herself, but you never know."

I knew it wasn't likely, but my heart still skipped a beat.

"Okay, let's go. Together," I said, and Tetsuo nodded.

*

I hadn't been on a night train in a while.

Tetsuo was fast asleep against the window in the seat opposite me, his long lashes cast down. In his school uniform, with his schoolbag and a plastic shopping bag in the wire rack overhead, he looked like an exhausted runaway.

Thinking back, I felt like he and I had always stopped just seeing each other as members of the opposite sex, using the fact that we were siblings simply as an excuse to be good to each other. When our parents were out we'd linger at the table after dinner, taking our time over dessert and drinking tea. The time we could spend alone together had always felt incredibly sweet.

The feeling had always seemed to be mutual.

Now that we were alone again, it felt all the stronger.

Shining lights sped past through the dark outside the window. Each time the train stopped and the doors opened, tendrils of the still, cold night streamed into the carriage. Gradually, the darkness deepened, and I looked up at the distant moon feeling somewhat uncertain, feeling like I was a long way from home.

But my mind was no longer clamoring for my attention. No matter how the wind rattled at the window or how swiftly the scenery flew past, even if an enigmatic night lay in wait all through the quiet carriage, I'd never again be driven by the overwhelming sense that there was something I needed to recall. I was fulfilled by the knowledge and the comfort of having found myself. Someday, somewhere up ahead, tonight would only be another scene from a long-ago dream. I wondered at the strangeness of it. I gazed at Tetsuo.

He's so adorable when he's asleep. Just look at how long his eyelashes are, I thought.

He looked like a slumbering god.

We arrived at Karuizawa sooner than I expected. Tetsuo must have been really tired: he'd woken up just once, glanced at his trusty workbooks, and then gone back to sleep until I shook him awake saying, "It's the next stop."

Where the hell am I? his face clearly said, before moving through a whole series of expressions as his brain caught up with the train of events that had led us here. It was hilarious to watch.

Then we stepped off the train onto the platform. The station was dark and discomfiting, with a stiff wind that seemed to rebuke us for coming here. An incredible number of stars twinkled above our heads, and the pale glow of the Milky Way crested the mountains and flowed across the sky.

We found a taxi and hurried north on the winding road that climbed toward Onioshidashi. The driver looked us up and down—a pair of young travelers arriving so late at night. We passed the big Seibu, hunkering quietly in the darkness, and got out of the car.

The cabins stood among the trees, regularly shaped and spaced out at intervals, as dark as tombs. The small homes were difficult enough to tell apart in the daytime, but at night they became even more featureless, retreating into the dark. Each one seemed familiar, and we walked around and around like Hansel and Gretel through the trees in near-total darkness and the smell of damp soil.

Night deepened, and we walked past countless unlit windows. We were both wondering whether this had been a hopeless quest, but wary of making it true by putting it into words, we kept our uncertainty from each other, and racked our brains for any distinguishing features that the family cabin would have had.

"What shape was the porch . . . ?"

"Pretty standard, I think."

"How about the gate? Was there a nameplate?"

"Um . . . Oh. The mailbox," Tetsuo said. "There was a cool green mailbox standing by the road, wasn't there?"

"Yes!" The mailbox suddenly appeared among the fragments of memory I'd been trying to trace—the shape of the kitchen sink in the cabin, the view from the window in the old-fashioned living room upstairs, the color of the sofa. "Like you'd see in a magazine! Dad had it sent all the way from America, and the first time it rained, it went rusty."

"That's it, got it. Okay. Stay right here until I come back."

Tetsuo continued quickly up the slope. I sat down on my

duffel and looked up at the encroaching darkness and the shadows of the trees. Through their branches I could see the moon and stars, looking strangely brilliant in the cold, and the bright white clouds cutting across them. And the pleasant scent of the forest—I'd loved this view and this smell since long before people started going forest bathing. I felt like the overhanging boughs were all watching over me, and even in such a dark night I felt glad. Although I was so much older now, the trees were still tall, just like they had been when I was a child, and that pleased me.

Before too long, Tetsuo came sprinting back. "Found it!"

"You're the best," I said, without thinking. But I meant it.

"I do this kind of thing all the time," he said, laughing.

Come to think of it, he often went off to the forest or the river and stayed out for several days at a time. Having learned the basics of life through playing sports, he knew how to respond to real-life situations with strength and resilience. My aunt had called it *understanding more than he thinks he knows*, and I knew exactly what she meant. The realization suddenly made me feel desperate to see her, even though I'd been with her just last night.

I followed Tetsuo to a lot with a rusty iron mailbox standing behind a crumbling fence. Now that I was here, I definitely recognized the family cabin. It looked pitch dark inside.

"Maybe she isn't here," I said.

"Let's go inside and find out. Do you remember where the key was?"

"I do."

I remembered. The potted plant that had been growing beside the front door had shriveled and died, but I plucked the spare key from under it and opened the door.

"Let's go see."

"Okay."

We stepped into the creaking darkness of the entryway, only the faint moonlight to guide us. Luckily though, the light in the hallway was working, and as soon as we found the switch, the space lit up.

"You check down here. I'm going upstairs," Tetsuo said, climbing up the stairs to the second floor, turning lights on one after the other.

There was an overwhelmingly musty smell. I opened each window I came across as wide as it would go, letting in the night air. The cold raced around the room, laden with fresh oxygen.

I opened the windows in the kitchen and then the living room that connected to it, and approached the room beyond. Nervously, I opened the sliding doors. It smelled of darkness and tatami, but the room was empty. I breathed out and walked over to the window, and opened it, too.

Right then, it came to me. I was sure my aunt had stood exactly where I was standing just recently—around the time of evening when the navy-blue sky, which the sun had almost departed, had backlit the profiles of the trees in intriguing mosaics. She stood here alone without the lights on, gazing out the window. I could feel it as clearly as though I held it in my hand. And she was gone. I didn't know where she'd gone, but she wasn't here anymore. In the clear night smell that was filling the room, I had no choice but to know it. Where was she? Maybe the need to try to find her wasn't quite as urgent as I'd thought. But it was my turn to look for her—this game we were playing was of the utmost importance. That much seemed clear.

After several minutes, I heard Tetsuo stomping down the stairs, bringing me back to reality. I switched the light on as he came down the hallway toward me.

He said, "She's not here, but there's this," holding out a piece of paper in my direction. "It was on the glass table in the upstairs living room," he said. I took the piece of paper and looked at it. In an untidy scrawl, it said:

> Dearest Yayoi,
> I can't believe you came. How nice of you!
> Distance really does make our hearts grow fonder.
> Yukino

No matter how many times I turned the paper over in my hands, there were no more clues to be gleaned from it. The trail had gone cold.

Tetsuo put his head to one side and said, "I feel like if this is all you're going to write, why write anything at all?"

This struck me as funny. I laughed and said, "I don't know. I think I can see what she means."

"I guess so," Tetsuo said, and laughed, too.

I felt a weight lift off my mind.

We were terribly hungry, but everything within walking distance was closed, and without a car we couldn't go farther out. Cursing our rash belief that all we needed to do was make it here, we turned the kitchen inside out in search of something to eat.

We found a couple of old cup noodles in a cupboard, and a large tub of yogurt and one tomato my aunt must have left behind in the refrigerator. They didn't fill us up, but after eating them we felt reassured, somehow, and said good night and awkwardly went into our separate rooms, like we were back at home. But of course we did. We were hardly going to start going to bed together now.

I got under the covers in the dark inside a night that was almost terrifyingly still.

I dreamed about my aunt. She knew everything, and was standing outside this cabin, looking up at the sky. Her head was tilted so far back that her hair almost reached the ground. I saw her standing there, with a slightly standoffish profile, singing sweetly to the stars.

It was a poignant dream.

The next day was the kind of beautiful day that Karuizawa was famous for.

I made the most of it by cleaning the cabin. Tetsuo had suggested that we could go see some of the sights this afternoon, even if we were going back home to Tokyo today. We phoned my aunt's house repeatedly, but no matter how long we let it ring, she didn't pick up. She wasn't back yet.

I was scrubbing the floor in the hallway when the doorbell rang. In the unfamiliar house, the doorbell sounded hesitant, as though I'd only imagined the sound. I looked up and froze, but it rang again, twice, echoing in the entryway.

I walked over to the door, expecting it to be Tetsuo. I'd let him go shopping to his beloved big Seibu, but now that I thought about it, it was probably closed in the off-season. So he must have had to go farther away, in which case it was still too early for him to be back.

I stood in front of the door and said, "Who's there?"

"Is that you, Yukino?" the person said.

It was a young male voice. From the urgency I could hear in it, I intuited that he'd probably come here looking for her, too.

So I opened the door.

I was shocked at just how young he was. He looked my age at most, possibly younger. *Oh, no, she's gotten involved with one of her students*, I thought. Of course she'd think nothing of it. Anyway, he was a young giant: tall, well-built, with a large head. I'd been looking up at him at a loss for words, and he was looking down at me with a very odd expression. It was the kind of expression you might have if you bumped into an old girlfriend on the street.

After we stood there staring at each other for several long seconds, he abruptly introduced himself.

"Oh, nice to meet you. My name is Masahiko Tatsuno. I'm sorry, but is Yukino . . . ?"

"She's not here," I said. "I'm Yayoi, her niece. Please, come in and have a cup of tea or something. I'd love to talk to you, if you don't mind. We—my brother and I were hoping to find her here, too."

"I see."

He was visibly disappointed at finding out my aunt wasn't here. He thought for a while, then said quietly, "Thank you, I'd be glad to stop in."

He seemed to be a stranger to ambivalence, or in-between expressions, and was almost uncannily polite. He reminded me of a samurai in a historical drama. Once he took a seat on the small sofa in the living room adjoining the kitchen, he looked like even more of a giant. He took a sip of green tea and sighed deeply.

"I got a call from her yesterday afternoon," he said. "I hadn't heard from her in three months. When I asked her where she was, she reeled off the address and then hung up after pretending to fumble with the phone. I'd made a note of the address, but then I saw where it was and got here as fast as I could. And how about you?"

"I've been staying with her for a while. So when she left without saying anything, I thought she might have come here . . . But she'd disappeared already, leaving nothing but a note behind for me. I have no idea where she is now. I've tried calling her house, but she's not there, or at least not picking up."

"Did she leave a note for me?" he said, his eyes lighting up in hope.

Apologetically I said, "She didn't."

He looked down again, sadly.

"You said it had been three months," I said. "So you haven't seen her recently?"

"That's right." It seemed like the whole story was ready to come tumbling out of him. "More accurately, she wouldn't see me. Perhaps she'd dumped me, to put it bluntly. So much happened that I don't really understand. We were only really together last year, when I was still in high school."

I knew it, I thought. He must have been her student. It seemed like exactly the kind of thing she would do.

"She said we could meet again once I graduated, so I called her three months ago. And she told me she . . . " For the first time, he hesitated. "She'd had an abortion, and it was ours."

I was taken aback. Not that I expected her to, but she hadn't breathed a word of it to me. Nothing about her had even suggested she was seeing someone.

"I felt I had to meet and talk to her at all costs, but she wouldn't do it. I tried everything, waited everywhere, but she refused to meet me."

He looked truly worn out. I was starting to understand that once my aunt had landed on a course of action, she'd stick to it no matter what. I shivered inwardly just imagining how chilly she could turn toward a partner once she was sure she didn't want to see them anymore. No doubt she'd have spoken to Masahiko like he was the person who came to read the gas meter. He must have a considerable stubborn streak himself to have clung on these three months in the face of it.

"Wait, if she said you could meet after you graduated, does that mean you broke up before that?" I asked.

"That's right. Last December, on a night when it was pouring down with rain, she summoned me and told me she wouldn't see me anymore. It was a bolt from the blue. There was nothing I could say or do to get her to listen—all she'd tell me was, *You're still in high school* . . . Looking back, she would have been pregnant then. But she likes to make her own decisions," he said.

What is this strange earnestness he has? I wondered. *It must be part of what she cherishes about him.*

"I'm back," Tetsuo said, coming through the door. Seeing Masahiko, he stopped in surprise.

I quickly outlined the situation to him.

Once he had introduced himself properly, Tetsuo said to me

in a low voice, "People keep coming out of the woodwork like it's some kind of detective novel. We could have a murder on our hands soon."

Somehow, I was so tickled I had to giggle under my breath, so Masahiko wouldn't hear.

*

There was something I always craved when I visited the mountains: Mom's fruit curry. Years ago when Dad used to drive us up here, the first thing we'd do was clean the house together. Then, for dinner the first night, Mom would make a sweet curry with kiwi and pineapple.

This time, I was the one cooking.

Tetsuo and I had been planning to return to Tokyo today, but Masahiko was insistent that she might come back to the cabin, since she'd given him the address. Tetsuo and I both thought this was unlikely, but taking pity on how hurt and exhausted he seemed, we decided to stay with him. In the absence of a next move, we were in no rush. So we made a strange crew as we sat down at the table for dinner.

"Yep, tastes the same as I remember. Just like Mom used to make," Tetsuo said.

"It's very nice," Masahiko said.

Tetsuo had always been good at being himself around strangers. The reason being he didn't really care what anyone thought. Between big mouthfuls of curry, he started questioning Masahiko voraciously.

"You're obviously built like an athlete. Sharp features.

Classic dresser. You wouldn't be short of nice girls to choose from, so I can't help but wonder: Why Aunt Yukino? I have to say I don't really see it. What is it you find attractive about her?"

He got into this kind of mischievous mood sometimes. At family gatherings he'd often say something outrageous and make everyone freeze. Masahiko could have played the question off with a joke, but being a serious kind of person he said:

"Yukino's incredibly true to herself. She knows who she is, and can't compromise on it—no matter what it costs her, or how difficult it is. It's clumsy, and hard to watch, but it's incredibly attractive. Plus, her class was fun."

"Music class?" I frowned.

"Yes. She's great. Once, when we had a singing test, the whole class played a prank and pretended we'd lost our voices."

He seemed to be keeping a kind of formal distance with me, for whatever reason. So I responded similarly, and said, "I see."

"I had a terrible cold that day, and genuinely couldn't sing. But when I told her that, all the other bastards in the class said the same thing. So she got up from her piano and said, 'It seems like there's a cold going around.' All of us cheered, because we thought the test was off. But she said, 'All of you who didn't sing, come up here,' and made the ones who'd pretended to be sick line up in front of the class. Including me, of course. We were all having fun, because we liked her. Then she said, 'Everybody open your mouth,' and so the dozen of us standing there opened our mouths like idiots. And she looked into each one and smiled and said, 'He's the only one telling the truth.

The rest of you are fine.' And she touched my neck. I've never been more flustered in my life. Then she snapped her handbag open and gave me a cough drop. It was amazing, the whole class clapped. She's special. That was in my senior year, and that was the day I started to like her."

Every man in love thinks his partner is special, but I thought I knew what he meant.

"I get it," Tetsuo said. "I can just imagine what her class must be like. I bet it's wild."

"It's pretty unconventional," Masahiko said, smiling almost proudly. "She wouldn't come to school if it was raining. When she's supposed to be the teacher! And sometimes she'd be ten minutes late to class, or leave early, so it was kind of exciting never knowing what would happen. Once, the piano suddenly went quiet, and we all wondered what was going on, but when we looked she'd fallen asleep."

"Wow," I said.

"She always gave us the questions before a test. She'd say, 'Just between us . . .' So we all got As, or near enough. Even in a performance test, she'd get people singing and go stare out the window. But she could suddenly get all serious, or be playful and feed me candy—she was never boring, anyway, and that's why she was popular. I always looked forward to music class after that. I was in love. And she was, too. I always knew—when we passed each other in the hallway, or if I was asleep in class and opened my eyes and found her looking at me from the piano, I knew . . . It's the happiest I've ever been. Loving her was the best," he said, narrowing his eyes like he was looking at something beautiful on the horizon, or talking about treasure. Maybe finding fellow travelers at the end of his long journey had put him in a sharing mood.

"Yeah, I can definitely see how someone else wouldn't be the same, once you got a taste of her," Tetsuo said.

I stayed quiet thinking of my aunt and her slow smile, its delicate glow. The night came in, bringing us dreams of someone who wasn't here. I felt like we'd been sitting here talking about her for years. At the bottom of this peaceful dream, we were gathered in a comfortable, brightly lit room, opening up equally to one another, filled with a spirit of trust. It was a rare kind of night. The moods of our hearts, the tone of the wind, the number of stars blinking in the sky, the measure of our melancholy, the tiredness in our limbs—all of these were in perfect balance, as though by a miracle.

"My mom was my dad's mistress," Masahiko said.

It was so out of nowhere, Tetsuo and I didn't know what to say. Masahiko smiled wryly at us gawping and went on. He seemed unashamed of what he was telling us, and I admired that.

"It's all in the past now. After she died, I was taken in by my dad's side of the family, and lived a normal life. Just a lucky spoiled kid. Trust me on this, but I would know. And ever since I turned old enough to be interested in girls, I'd always get with people who were what you'd call—bubbly. Do you know what I mean?" He turned to Tetsuo.

Tetsuo laughed, and said, "Yeah, I do. You look exactly like the type."

"I've been thinking about it, and I've come to believe that must have been a concern for Yukino. I thought I'd just been rejected, but I'm not sure that's it. And yeah, part of me wants a girl who's outgoing, and honest, and responsible, and acts her age, and shows her feelings, that kind of thing. That's what I've grown up looking for, and it always worked out pretty well before. But the important thing is the part I've left behind. The part I can't share with anyone."

When he said that, it gave me a start. I thought I'd heard something with the ring of truth whistle past my ear.

"There are years lying asleep inside me that I've forgotten entirely. A period of time when, as a little boy, I tried to protect my mom . . . When I was strong, but not strong enough. I'm not hung up on it or blaming anyone, but the part of my life when I lived with her turned into something I could never share, which I carried around all these years. At least I think I did. Because it only came back to me when I met Yukino. She was everything that was old and familiar, that I missed, that I regretted. It used to drive me crazy seeing her coming toward me across the schoolyard in the rain with her umbrella—everything it reminded me of."

"I think that's pretty normal when you're in love," Tetsuo said, and it was obvious to me that it rubbed Masahiko the wrong way. Hastily, I tried to say something, but Tetsuo continued, calmly and clearly:

"I thought it was just another case of a teacher who should know better and a boy looking for a mother figure, but the way you talk about it, I feel like I'm getting to know her a little."

Masahiko gave him a genuine smile, and said, "Thanks."

I was very glad to see it.

Because, of course, the same thing had brought me here—not the fact that she was my sister, or because she'd disappeared without a word. But the dark feminine magic that was her nature. Behind her hair, her sweet ringing voice, her long fingers on the piano, she harbored something vast, lost, and familiar, and it was like a siren call to those of us who were missing parts of our childhoods. It was something deeper than night, longer than eternity, out of reach.

We saw her in our minds, bearing this burden for so long, how she stayed true, her courage and grace, the pain it must have caused. And then, ever more enthralled, we end up coming together like this in a starry wood to share a meal.

That's how it goes.

＊

Late that night, Tetsuo and I went on a walk.

In the pitch-black wood, between dark-windowed houses that rose like ghosts in the dark, through the faint rays of moonlight, we walked. Deep green air seemed to ripple out into the night sky every time the wind shook the trees' leafy, slumbering branches.

"What a weird kid! I can't believe he just told us all that, without even seeming embarrassed about it," Tetsuo said.

Since he hadn't brought a change of clothes, I'd lent him my cardigan, which was too short on him, and I thought he looked adorable.

"Yeah. But he's a good guy."

To me, Masahiko seemed to have been taken captive by a dream in which my aunt happened to appear. I wondered whether he'd ever make it out. But maybe that was what people called happiness. The more beautiful a night away from home was, the more regretful it made you feel. I looked up at the sky, trying to get a grip on my own existence before it vanished into the darkness. Under the summer constellations, we walked and walked.

"There are so many stars out here," Tetsuo said.

"How long do you think it's been since we were last here?"

"A good few years, right? I think Mom and Dad use it a lot, though."

"It's nice to be back. Everything looks smaller than I remember."

"The last time we were here, we'd just gotten the mailbox."

"We had fireworks."

"Yeah, I remember Dad carrying a bucket of water around. We always brought fireworks when we came up here."

As a child, I'd always been reduced to a kind of grief by the idea that each one of the bright shining dots that the sky seemed to brim with was an entire star. That the lights of billions of stars were contained in the spaces between the tree branches I looked up through.

"Why am I sad?" I'd asked Dad. "Does it make everyone feel like this?" We were climbing uphill toward a small clearing in the forest where we'd have the fireworks. Dad had a bucket in one hand, and was holding mine with the other. The darkness was so thick I thought we would lose sight of Mom, who was walking just ahead. Tetsuo, excited at getting to carry an armful of fireworks, had run ahead alone.

Dad said, "When people see too many of something, it just makes them feel sad. No one knows why."

I remember it clearly, even down to the texture of Dad's hand as I held it firmly to mine. The dad who raised me, and the palm of his big, dry hand.

Tetsuo and I made a good loop and were coming up to the home stretch. My eyes had acclimatized, and the trees in the forest appeared almost to glow, like images from a dream. Our cabin was just down the hill. Masahiko must still be up; I could see a distant light in the window. If we kept walking over the twigs and dry dirt toward its starlike beacon we'd be back in no time. The thought made me feel cold, as if the forest air were infiltrating the cells of my heart, one by one, and claiming them for the night.

"Yayoi," Tetsuo said suddenly. "What are you gonna do tomorrow?"

I stopped and stood still. Maybe I wasn't yet ready to go back inside. I looked up at the stars. No matter how many times I saw them, it was hard to believe just how crystalline the air was here tonight.

"What will I do . . . ? Me?" I didn't really want to think about it yet. "I want to find her, I guess. I don't want to give up now. But I guess I'll go back to her place. It doesn't seem likely she'll come back here."

It was an answer that didn't address anything of importance. I just didn't know. I felt as if I were looking into the depths of an infinite pool.

"Hey." Tetsuo sighed, and slid down the trunk of the tree he'd been leaning against until he was sitting on the ground. "So you want to go live with your real family? At this stage?"

My jaw fell open. I was caught so off-guard the stars seemed to whirl above me.

"You knew, Tetsuo? Since when?"

Gazing into the dark without looking at me, he said, "I've known for a long time. I think you're the last. Of course Mom and Dad don't know I know . . . So are you going to live with Aunt Yukino from now on?"

"No." I crouched in front of him and peered into his face. "The only home I have is the one I grew up in. Neither of us is that much of a dreamer. It's just . . . I don't want to miss out on a single piece of what it means that I finally remembered, and how she's my sister, and how that changes everything. I know I'm making people worry by running around like this right now. But I need to do this. If Yukino wants me to come after her, that's what I want to do. I think maybe stupid things like this are exactly what she and I need—what we needed. Does that make sense?"

"I totally get it," Tetsuo said, and smiled. He looked me in the eye and nodded. It was a beautiful smile, one that made you open your eyes wide, and all I could do was look. During this trip, I'd seen so many expressions he'd never shown me before. This smile was another. Maybe it was one he'd reserved for specific women until now, because I couldn't picture him with a smile like that at home . . . But no, it was probably my eyes that had changed. Tonight, after the last few days had stripped away all the filters that had been on it, my heart was seeing Tetsuo through brand-new eyes.

This new Tetsuo, these newborn feelings. I only had eyes for him. As if I were listening out for the smallest of sounds, I wanted never to turn away from the way he looked to me now.

"You always seemed lost," he said. "You shouldn't have known, but whether we were at home or out, you always looked worried, or restless. I got the idea when I was in middle school that Aunt Yukino wasn't really our aunt, and that you and her were sisters, so I went to city hall and looked up the family register. You were both adopted into our family."

". . . Oh."

The ground and the leaves by my feet were faint in the moonlight. I knew we'd reached the end of something.

"I only found out by accident."

I felt like we were talking about something very unhappy. Every word that came out of my mouth seemed as white and cold as the stones on the shore of the mythical Sanzu River which led to the afterlife. I felt distant, in every dimension, from where hearts beat and blood flowed, from things like life and death, and home and family . . . and love, and Tetsuo.

"Honestly, though, I'm pretty happy about it. Isn't it like getting two lives? It's always better to know than not know. I'm sure of that."

The night breeze drifted, and while my words were truthful, I knew they were also slipping away from something else. The easy, familiar clasp of my fingers on my knees as I squatted on the ground might have been the only thing that was holding steady.

Then it happened.

Tetsuo took me in his arms. I fell forward onto my knees, but strangely, I wasn't surprised. The shell buttons on the front of the cardigan he was wearing were suddenly up against my face. I noticed the unexpected sensation of Tetsuo's big hands against my back. He smelled of home. Of the house where I grew up; its beams, its clothes, its furnishings. And instead of confusing me, it filled me with so much longing that I thought I might cry. So, instead, I raised my head and looked into his diamond eyes. They were shining so sorrowfully that I had to close my eyes. Our lips met. It was a kiss that seemed to last as long as eternity.

*

There are some actions you take that change everything. The kiss was one of those.

Afterward, we stood up without saying a word, dusted ourselves off, and walked to the cabin. We smiled a little as we said good night and went to our separate bedrooms.

I failed to get to sleep.

I felt as though I'd lost my bearings—like I was alone seeing off a ship sailing away into darkness. Still, my heart pulsed with a somber longing. It was a sweet-tasting darkness. Without meaning to, I kept thinking only of Tetsuo's lips, the way his chest felt against my cheek when he pulled me to him.

I was as sure of it as I was of anything in this world, and there was nothing I wasn't ready to give up in return. But I felt as bereft as if I were face-to-face with the absolute darkness of the universe. There was nowhere for us to go, no tomorrow where we could be together. Just now, at the bottom of a night so clear, the two of us were feeling the same way, but it might all melt away like a dusting of snow when the sun came up.

I didn't have the strength to picture a happy ending for us.

Yes, my heart was exhausted. Until the moment when I could be reunited with my aunt, I needed everything else to wait.

Quietly, I just kept thinking to myself what I knew Tetsuo had to be thinking, too: *We've done it now. We've finally done it.*

*

The morning dawned gray and overcast, and I was looking out the window at the forest watching the cold air, as fine as mist, flow slowly through the trees.

I hadn't gotten much sleep.

From where I lay between the smooth new sheets, the cloudy highland sky looked very pretty. I gave up on sleep and opened the sliding doors and walked down the hallway. The cabin was as quiet as a dream of an old country house. I went to the kitchen. Starting the day with leftover curry felt like conceding defeat, so I decided to fix some breakfast. I was feeling foggy. As of late, every day had been so long and so filled with things that nothing seemed to have landed.

Barefoot on the chilly floor, I filled the kettle with the startlingly cold water, then lit the stove. I was looking into the fridge to see what there was when Masahiko came in.

"Good morning," he said. It was still early, but he was neatly dressed and looked awake.

"Morning. Have you been out?" I said.

"Yes, I went for a walk."

He smiled and went to sit on the couch in the living room. I knew that the difference in their lifestyles, which to anyone else would have seemed endearing, would have terrified my aunt. Rather than their age gap, or her ethics as a teacher, her horror of his wholesomeness would have held her back, almost like they were two people from completely different planets. She was fearful of having to change her narrow, untidy life. I thought I knew exactly how she must have felt. It seemed far too likely that their relationship was a youthful whim for Masahiko, and that once the whirlwind of falling in love had passed, he would go back to his normal life. Any way you looked at it, she was unlikely to make a serious partner for anyone.

Feeling like my aunt's weaknesses as a person had become visible to me for the first time, I felt a little sorrowful. She had a habit of looking away from things she feared, or found distasteful, or thought might hurt her. I was thinking about the umbrella stand.

The day I arrived at my aunt's and asked to stay, I'd folded my umbrella up and stuck it in the umbrella stand in the entrance hall without thinking much of it. The stand was a plain pot, and quite an old one at that. A couple of days later, it was raining again, so I pulled out my umbrella and almost dropped it in shock: it was completely covered in mildew. Alarmed, I rushed up to my aunt's room. She'd taken the day off from school and was asleep in bed. I picked my way across the clothes-strewn floor and woke her up.

"What is it?" She sat up sleepily.

"Have you looked inside the pot in the entrance hall recently? You should check it out. You won't believe it. My umbrella's totally covered in mildew."

"Oh, that? Yeah, I have a folding umbrella, so I never use it. Once you put something in there, you can't take it out again. I used to put umbrellas in it. It's true. So did something happen to yours?" she said in a murmur, groggily, her hair falling over her face.

"It's absolutely covered in mildew. I've never seen anything like it," I said, agitated.

My aunt watched the colorless drops of rain running down the window with a frown on her face.

Eventually, she said, "Okay. Let's forget it ever existed."

"What do you mean?" I said.

"Take the whole pot, with the umbrella and all, and throw it out in the yard. Then just stay inside for the day. It's raining, after all," she said, and retreated back under the covers.

I gave up and took the heavy pot around to the back of the house like I'd been told. Striding through wet weeds that came up to my knees, I saw the back of the ramshackle house for the first time. It was in total disrepair. On top of that, the yard was full of a hair-raisingly large pile of things that my aunt had previously decided to forget, abandoned to the rain. It was hard to even fathom how long she had been throwing things away there. All manner of things she had haphazardly tossed onto the pile so she could avoid having to look at or think about them ever again—even old stuffed animals, and an entire child's study desk and shelving unit, however she'd managed to get it out here. I imagined my aunt saying goodbye to people in the same categorical way, and started to feel a little despondent. I stood there in the rain looking at all the things that had been forgotten for quite some time.

*

"Are you making something?" Masahiko, whom my aunt might already have forgotten all about, called out from the living room.

Over the noise of washing vegetables, I said, "Yes, some breakfast."

"Can I help?" he said, getting up and coming over. "I've been taking advantage of your kindness."

"That's okay, I don't mind . . . Do you cook?"

I laughed at myself. I wasn't sure why I was being so formal with a boy my own age. But there was something about him that made you want to act properly. Whether this was just who he was, or because he had aged prematurely from going through a painful breakup, I'd treated him like he was much older than me from the beginning.

"Yes, it's one of my talents," he said, laughing.

"Then maybe I can ask you to take these," I said, and handed him a plastic colander full of snow peas I was going to put in the miso soup. He took them from me with a smile. As he sat cross-legged on the floor like a child, removing the strings with his big hands, I watched him with a feeling of amusement. He was evidently the kind of person who did nothing by halves.

"My late mother was always really sick. So by the time I was in elementary school, I'd cook dinner for both of us. Trying to think about nutrition, even as a child, to make sure she was eating well. So I'm an old hand."

"Oh, well, in that case, could you do this as well? It just needs chopping—however you like."

Preparing the stock, I got the spare cutting board and knife, and handed him the konnyaku in its plastic package. He'd finished the peas already, and took the knife with obvious relish. When I looked over after a while, he had sliced the konnyaku into neat strips with slits down the middle, and twisted them into little braids. It was frankly impressive.

"My aunt doesn't cook, does she?" I said.

"No, not at all. Does she not know how to keep house? Or does she just choose not to?" He laughed.

"I don't think she knows how," I said.

Yes, she had grown up a feral child in the city. She'd survived on her own in a cold home with no one there to stand in the kitchen, or take care of the cleaning and laundry, or mend things when they broke. Every time I thought of this lately, I felt my chest pierced through by a sharp pain. *If only I'd been a little older and smarter when the accident happened, so we could have lived together, then . . .* But our destinies had already diverged, and each of us had grown to adulthood by our own way. We couldn't go back. I tried to dismiss the feeling, telling myself it was junk—pure nostalgia, and disrespectful to both of our realities.

"She can barely use a can opener," Masahiko said, smiling

at the memory. "I'd often cook and get her to help with things, just like you're doing. It was hilarious to watch: she can't peel a potato or open a can, and she'll get sulky about it on top of that. I know it sounds like mommy issues, but I loved that about her. My mother used to boss me around, too, even though she was always in bed."

It's kind of tragic, I thought, *how we can never completely escape our childhoods*. The morning had fully arrived, and pale sunlight was coming in through the window. It illuminated my hands as I worked, and I felt my drowsy confusion get bundled away somewhere deep inside my head.

"Um," Masahiko said, suddenly serious, handing me a pile of neat konnyaku twists.

"Yes?" I said, taking the colander from him, and paused.

"I hope you don't mind me asking, but do you know she's . . . ?"

It seemed like it had been old news to everyone but me, and for a moment, I was sick of it all. I turned away from him to the sink and said, "I know. She's my sister."

Taken aback by my barbed tone, he immediately said, "I'm sorry."

Wait a second, I thought. *If he knows, he must have heard it from Yukino*. That seemed incredible to me.

I put a smile on my face, and said, "No, it's all right. But how do you know about it?"

"Yukino mentioned it," he said, clearly. "That she had a younger sister, but she couldn't live with her. I asked her where, but she'd say things like *over beyond the mountains*, or *somewhere in this world*, and not take me seriously. She'd stop herself every time she almost told me more. It was always on my mind, and yesterday, when I met you, I knew straight away that it was you."

"I see," I said, taking in what he'd said.

"She didn't tell me details," he said, his big dark eyes full of hope, "but when I was going over there regularly—well, there was no sign of her being in touch with this sister. And she wouldn't talk about her family. Her parents were dead, she had one sister, and they used to live in a house with a pond in the garden. That was it. Honestly, it worried me, but I feel better about it now. You've come all this way to find her, which means—she's not alone."

"Of course," I said. "I'll follow her anywhere, and I'll wait as long as it takes."

"Same here," he said, and smiled.

There was nothing self-abasing in Masahiko's smile. These days, when I was around him, or Tetsuo, or my aunt, I felt free of the vague and mysterious guilt that had been with me since I was a child. It was as though, along with the old truths that had been uncovered, the new me was finally getting to breathe real air. It felt good. *Hopefully he'll get to see her soon, whenever the timing's right for them to talk things through*, I thought. My aunt obviously trusted him already, and by then, the normal passing of time might have softened her heart toward him even more. And if so, then everything might turn out okay, and they might end up happy together.

Someday, he would fix up that terrifying house, calling a

waste truck to haul away the mountain of trash, and getting the windows and the gate repaired. The house would be reborn as their new home—a home where my aunt and Masahiko would live together, freely, just the way they liked. The garden would be tended to, and children would play on the sunny balcony. And if Tetsuo and I could go visit, but not as siblings, and if I could talk to my aunt as if we'd always been sisters . . . The vision seemed so out of reach, with so many obstacles between here and there, that it shone like something out of paradise. Of course, brightness wasn't everything, but the light was so blinding that it seemed unearthly, almost like a kind of prayer. And for a second, I felt it strongly: *This could be real.* There was nothing to stop a day like that happening in the future.

"The rice will be done in half an hour, and then we'll have breakfast," I said, leaving the kitchen.

My head was still foggy, and I thought I'd crawl back into bed for a while.

"Great, I'll set the table," Masahiko said, smiling.

*

As soon as we sat down for breakfast, both Tetsuo and I naturally reached inside ourselves and slipped back into our sibling dynamic. Since we'd spent years facing each other this way, it was a rock-solid foundation that let us avoid feeling embarrassed or awkward at all. We were more discreet than any clandestine affair could ever be—so much so that, even though I was playing dumb just as much as he was, I secretly felt a little miffed.

Once we got on the train back to the city, I sank into my seat and fell into a deep sleep, mouth hanging open. I slept through all the stops the train made, except once when I half woke up and overheard Tetsuo and Masahiko talking quietly.

Tetsuo was sitting next to me, and Masahiko was in the seat across from him. With my head leaning against the window, I listened drowsily to what they were saying.

"If you hear from her before I do, I'd like it if you'd let me know, even if she tells you not to. I won't cause any trouble. Please, would you do this for me? You're my only hope," Masahiko said.

Tetsuo, as a bystander to the situation, stayed quiet for a while. I could sense his hesitation through the warmth of his

104

leg, which was leaning lightly against mine. He'd never agree to something he couldn't promise to do.

"Okay. You got it," Tetsuo said. "What's your address?"

Masahiko swiftly wrote something down in a beautiful black notebook, tore out the page, and handed it to Tetsuo.

"It's gonna work out. Aunt Yukino's no fool. She'll probably get in touch again soon. Yeah, I think you can count on it," Tetsuo said, and smiled.

Masahiko turned to him with a light in his eyes and said, "The way you say it, I actually feel like it might come true."

Endless fields passed outside the train window, alternating patches of light and dark. With my eyes barely open I watched as the sun, floating in the corner of sky I could see, seemed to melt brilliantly into the shining clouds that moved across its face.

*

Ueno Station, where we stepped off the train at noon, was like a different country. I was still disoriented from sleep. Everything seemed to be bathed in a haze of pale sunlight.

Masahiko smiled brightly at Tetsuo and me as we said our goodbyes. Watching him walk away, wave back at us, and get swallowed up into the crowds of Tokyo, I suddenly saw how attractive he probably was. I was still incredibly sleepy. I felt unsteady on my feet, and the buzz of the crowd and the voice coming over the station PA seemed peculiarly colorless and far away. I walked through the station hiding behind Tetsuo like he was a shield. I wanted to get on a train and go home with my brother. To throw my heavy bag down on my bed, stick my laundry in the bathroom hamper, laugh about how tired we were as we ate dinner with the TV on, and talk to my parents and close the distance that had opened up between us while I'd been away. And then, to sleep. Sleeping soundly, I'd hear Tetsuo's footsteps coming down the hallway . . . I was homesick. My fantasy was so real it made me dizzy.

But I couldn't do it.

"Wanna get something to eat?" Tetsuo said. We were walking past the giant panda statue.

"I think so," I said. The crowd in the station was getting on my nerves, and making me feel even more drained.

"Let's get out of here."

"Yeah."

We exited through the turnstile and made our way through the park. The old buildings shone dully amid the greenery. The wind already had the bright smell of early summer. The trees along the road swayed in the wind and cast their faint shadows on the asphalt. Pleasant groups of people stood everywhere we looked in the great big park. We walked in silence.

The next time I see him, we'll be back home, I thought. When I imagined seeing him around the house as though nothing had changed, it was like a gust of wind blowing through my heart, and I became even more confused about what I should do. Love wasn't like anything else—it was a creature with a mind of its own. There was no stopping it now.

"Where to?" Tetsuo said, turning to me.

"Kurofune-tei," I said, naming a favorite yoshoku spot.

"Good call," he said, and started walking again. We went down the long stone steps into the city. The sound of traffic suddenly grew louder. I saw our reflection flash past in the glass frontages of the shops along the street, thinking that from the outside, we looked just like a couple back from a short vacation.

He can get back to studying for his exams, I thought, watching his shoulders sway along to his steps. I loved the way he walked. He always looked so confident that it made me feel a little lonely. His upright posture, his long, slightly turned-out stride, his wide shoulders and strong arms. I watched them in turn as we walked, and it felt like we were the only people in the world. Just for a minute I could forget about all the other people on the street, the cars, the crowded buildings, and even my aunt. There was only Tetsuo.

I'd never known a love before that could blot out the world around it like this.

*

All through our meal, I didn't say a word. Tetsuo sat with his elbows propped up on the table and seemed to have something on his mind, too. I tore my baguette slices into tiny pieces and ate them as slowly as I could. I wished we didn't have to finish eating.

"You're coming home, right?" Tetsuo said, suddenly.

"What? Not today," I said, surprised. He sounded like he was questioning me, or anxious, and it made him sound much younger.

"No, I mean after that," he said.

"Of course. Where else would I go?" I said. I felt my heart start thumping deep inside my chest.

Sitting squarely in his chair, still eating, Tetsuo said, "Then I'll leave once I get into college."

I stayed quiet.

"I'll pick a school that's far enough away that I have to move out. It might be a little complicated, but let's take it one step at a time. What do you think?"

I knew this was him telling me how he felt, after everything we'd done, and what that had given us. Now that he'd put it all on the table, I could no longer pretend it had just been a moment

109

of madness. He knew that. When there was something he really wanted, he knew how to speak to people so they'd listen. That was how he'd gotten everything he wanted up to now. But now that he was turning his powers of persuasion onto me for the first time, of the many layers of emotion in my heart, what responded was deeper than sisterly, or even womanly.

It was a sense of pity, or something close to it. I felt a little sorry for him.

It pained me: *All the love our parents gave you, and I'm the one you want?* I took hold of his hand that was lying on the table. He looked at mine in surprise. I hadn't planned on it, but his hand in mine felt firm and warm, just like when we were kids.

"I can leave."

I meant it. *It could work out*, I thought. I'd move in with my aunt. Living with her, the dark hallways, the sound of the trees, and the wind moving through the night. Her sweet profile, the music of the piano, the weeping moon, the light on fragrant green mornings . . . Images of that future appeared before my eyes, and I welcomed them. It was a good future, in its way. I even knew exactly how I would feel there with my aunt. It must have been a dream belonging to my other self. But that me had already lost her chance to live this life.

As if to prove it, Tetsuo said, "No, you stay."

I swallowed, and looked at him. Tetsuo looked sad. "Don't get it twisted. Me moving out is not the same as you running away from this."

"I know," I said. I could tell he was scared.

He gulped down his water, and said, "This time when you

left, I couldn't stand it. Of course Mom and Dad must have been upset, too, but I was so worried I thought I was going to go out of my mind."

I'd seen a lot of people bare their souls around here lately—not just out of a desire to be truthful, but with courage and intention. Me included. And even if it was just a momentary flash, or something that might soon pass, the faith that could be entrusted to a single, all-encompassing look had the power to move hearts.

Keeping his eyes on me, Tetsuo said, "Everything I did up to now, I did to distract myself from my thoughts about you. Well, sometimes the distractions kind of turned into the main attraction. But you were never just my sister. More like an older girl who hung out in my house. Since the beginning. I've never seen you any other way. Because I knew this whole time. If you'd never found out, then I could probably have stayed your brother forever. People do that all the time. But for whatever reason, you started to remember. Mom started acting weird, and then you left a few days later, so I knew this time it was for real."

"This time?" I said.

"A long time ago—I couldn't help myself," Tetsuo said, and smiled. "You used to leave a lot. It must have been a couple of years ago, when you were gone for three days. I called Aunt Yukino's house."

I started smiling, too. It was funny just picturing it.

"I was so nervous, and I don't know why but I got it into my head and panicked. Like, *She knows . . . She knows, and she's*

never coming back. So I phoned her and said, 'Is Yayoi there?'
I thought my heart was going to burst from the anticipation
of it finally happening, you know? Then she says, '. . . Why?'
and it was funny, and so embarrassing. I knew I'd jumped the
gun, and didn't know what to say, and she giggled and said
'Bye,' and hung up, and I knew I was busted. You know that
way she has of just magically knowing things? . . . Now that it's
actually happened, maybe I was prepared, but it's no big deal. I
should have saved myself all the angst."

"It only happened," I said, the words tumbling out of my
mouth, "because you came to Karuizawa. I don't think it would
have. If we didn't go there together."

". . . Probably. Things turned out so well, I almost feel like
it was all a dream," Tetsuo said.

His smiling eyes were soft. I was watching Tetsuo and taking in the beauty of the color of the orange juice in front of me
at the same time. A sparkling romantic emotion, highly con-
centrated and yet also fresh, lay in the small space between us.

"We're not going stir crazy just because summer's around
the corner, are we? We've always been this way?" I said. I
wanted to make sure.

Ever since we were kids.

Every time I thought of anyone else.

I'd been disappointed they weren't him.

"You're ridiculous," Tetsuo said, smiling.

"That's good. It's going to be good," I said, and he said, "Of
course it is."

We were in love, but he smiled at me again, looking like my

brother. It felt almost intolerably bittersweet. He'd been wait-ing all this time. Living in the same house, pretending not to know anything, waiting for this to happen.

We parted ways at the station. I got on a train to my aunt's, and Tetsuo headed home.

Tetsuo said "See ya," as usual, and went down the stairs without looking back. For just a moment, I watched him go. His back was tall, and he swung his arms confidently at each step.

I could have seen with my eyes closed exactly how he'd stride onto the train, his head looking straight ahead above the curve of his spine, how he'd sit down on the seat, the expression on his face as he'd look out the window. The three days we'd been at each other's side still echoed in my chest like a distant afterimage. I could feel the satisfaction of a sweet, painful con-summation flowing quietly along the bottom of my heart.

*

I was dog-tired, but my heart was wide awake. So I knew as soon as I looked up at my aunt's house, which was lit up by the warm sunshine, that she wasn't there. I'd half expected it, but it was still a blow. I didn't know what to do.

I walked up to it anyway, unlocked the door, turned the brass knob, and stepped into the silence inside the house. The whole house was muted and quiet, like it was the middle of the night. I sighed deeply and went to put my duffel in my room. Then I got out a fresh set of clothes and took a hot shower.

I sat down in the tub and let the water wash away every last drop of my exhaustion. Under the stream of hot water, I closed my eyes and thought dimly: *What now? Sleep?* But the image that kept coming to me was the sight of my aunt. And the scene I couldn't turn my mind's eye away from was her sitting at the kitchen table in the cabin . . . She must have written the note there. I saw her clearly. She was writing to me in a rush, her hair falling on the table. Writing to me, thinking of me, wondering whether I'd come looking for her . . . I felt desperate to put an end to her journey. *If I don't stop her now, she's going to keep doing this forever,* I thought. I wanted her to know she could have more than this.

I was calling out to her from within the embrace of the warm vapor. My vision was clouded, and my limbs felt overheated and listless. I thought I had done everything I could, but even as I sat there with my wet hair, my heart was still searching for her.

After I got out of the bath, I decided to try one last time and opened the door to my aunt's room. The heat of the shower had gone to my head, but I still had an inkling that I might find something I'd missed before.

The room was still as messy as I'd last seen it, with nowhere to put my feet. The air had gone stale, and the whole room was oppressively warm. I opened the window to let in the bright afternoon breeze. The air, which had been as thick as darkness, escaped through the window all at once.

I cast my mind back to the first time I'd ever been in this room. I was still in elementary school, and it was winter, and my aunt was playing the piano. *When did I last hear . . .* It was just a few days ago, while I'd been asleep. That night, she played this piano to herself, went to bed, and . . . No, maybe she didn't. Then she went on a journey. She turned her drawers upside down, stuffed her things in a bag, and simply had to leave. To run away from facing me the next morning as her sister. I walked over to the piano. A big piano, like you'd find in a music room, and a comfortable-looking wooden chair. I didn't know how to play, but I sat down at it and lifted the heavy lid, and pressed down on the ivory-colored keys. A deep, round tone rang out cleanly in the house's silence.

As I closed the lid and stood up, I spotted a small book on the floor by the back leg of the piano.

There.

Why hadn't it occurred to me until now? I picked the book up like a priceless treasure, and then I was sure. The book was a guidebook to Aomori. That day, my aunt had said with a faraway look in her eyes . . . *Our last family vacation. We went up to Aomori.*

She'd probably had no intention of going there at first. Perhaps she'd realized some things in Karuizawa, after she'd impulsively called Masahiko. And then, unable to resist . . . The guidebook was dog-eared on the page for Osorezan, the volcano with a sacred site on the shore of its crater lake. It was a very old book that must have belonged to our father. Someone had noted down a hotel telephone number, some day itineraries, and other details in an adult hand. I stared hard at the letters marked in scratchy fountain pen, and softly stroked the book, which smelled of old paper. *This is my father*, I thought to myself. *His handwriting. Marks he left that prove he was really here.*

I went out of the room with the book carefully cradled against my chest. I knew I had it this time. If I followed the itinerary and found the hotel, I would definitely find her. I dragged my bag out again and went downstairs to find the phone ringing.

Whoever was calling, it had to be important. I ran to the kitchen and grabbed the clamoring receiver off its hook.

"Hello?"

It was Mom. All of a sudden, I felt like bursting into tears. Her voice soaked into my tired head, beyond reason or circumstance. It was the same voice that had picked up on the other end of the line the first time I stayed out all night, and the winter day I found out I'd failed my college entrance exams. For a second, Mom's voice took me right back there.

"Mom?" I said. My throat felt dry.

"Oh, Yayoi! I thought I'd call and find out what you were up to. Get yourself together and come back soon. Dad's in a major sulk."

Mom said it cheerfully, without betraying any hint of what she must have been through recently, or how she was feeling.

Then she said, "How's Yukino?"

"Yeah," I said. "She's, um, out shopping right now. I can take a message."

"No, that's okay. It's you I wanted. You'd better come home soon. Okay?"

I could vividly picture her face, the spot where she was standing in the hallway, even the wood grain on the wall.

"I'll be back in two or three days, I promise. I'm sorry. I'm done here. I've had a good time," I said.

Maybe this time, and every time, I did nothing but bring her pain. On the other end of the line, I heard the door shut and Tetsuo call out, "I'm home."

"Okay, well, we can't wait," my mom said, quietly.

"Yeah, I'll be back soon," I said, and hung up.

To shake off the lingering echo, which seemed only to remind me of my loneliness, I got up and hurried to the front door. I slung my bag over my shoulder and made for the station. The sun was still high, and the cloudy sky was so bright it stung my eyes.

I was off to Aomori.

*

Through the dull light, the bullet train bound for Morioka steadily went on overtaking the unfamiliar scenery stretching away from it on both sides.

I was so physically exhausted that I slept for most of the journey. No matter how many times I woke up, I seemed to be no nearer to my destination.

I'll find her this time.

I was sure of it. I was on my way to her now, and everything else could fall by the wayside. All the senses of my sleepy body were open and ready, and it was an oddly pleasurable feeling.

No, I didn't know what was going to happen. But the present was simply sweet. *It's enough*, I thought. The anchors were raised, the sails hoisted—so just for now I could take in the beauty of the waves and sky and be happy. That was allowed.

When I got back home, all my favorite food would be waiting on the dinner table, and Dad would be there, too, even if it meant he had to leave work early. Mom would make me clean my room and tell me all about the flowers that had come into bloom while I was gone. It wouldn't be long before we settled back into our old groove. And the changes that had happened within me would get subsumed into the process of me growing up. *It's really true*, I thought. *It's always better to know than not know.*

I was deeply relieved. I finally had the sense that everything would be okay. The confidence that I could take matters into my own hands and put them right had been totally missing from my life lately, when it seemed I'd been feeling my way through the dark blindfolded. Now, it was all mine. The view from the window as we sped farther north shone dimly, like a dream. My body, sunk into the seat, was transfixed. The sound of the rails ringing faintly through the sparsely peopled carriage mingled with the conversations of the other passengers and trickled evenly into the depths of my ears. *I'm going to be on this train forever* . . . I thought. I felt like the rhythm of the moving train might be soaking into my body in some indelible way. I might have been dozing, or I might have seen it with waking eyes. But having spent so many days thinking only of the past, and after my encounter with my real father's handwriting earlier . . .

I was starting to truly remember.

*

"We're going to Aomori tomorrow. You can put some things in here if you want."

My sister holds out a red backpack with her skinny arms. I was looking forward to the trip, of course. But I'd never experienced an evening so miserable. I was plunged in a sorrow so deep, it makes me shudder just to recall it. Lonely and fearful, I clung to my mother as she combed her hair. I wanted to grab hold of everything with my tiny fists and never let go. I had no way of staving off the misery that just kept welling up inside me.

"Okay, okay. All right. I'll ask Yayoi to do it for me," my mother said, smiling. Yes, she spoke slowly. With my ear pressed against her back, I could feel the deep resonance of her beautiful voice. My clumsy fingers gathered her long, sweetly scented hair into a braid. I could see in the mirror that she was smiling.

"Where's Daddy?" I asked, totally beside myself that he wasn't there. The tatami mats in the room were shabby, and there was a wide veranda. I was watching the garden and the pond glinting in sunken colors in the glare of the westerly light.

"He went to get provisions for our trip. He's going to get us all kinds of things we don't need. He might bring back something for you, too, Yayoi. He hasn't been shopping in a while," my mother said.

But I didn't feel happier. "If only he'd come back soon," I said, finding myself tearing up for some reason. The foreknowing was very much like that autumn sunset. It was as though the angled rays of the sun were illuminating things lying deep within my chest.

"Dear child, what are you crying about?" my mother said, cupping my cheeks in her hands, looking like she might cry herself. Even more helpless to stop my hot tears, I started to sob.

My mother hugged me tight and gently said, "What happened?" Her kindness was so pure that when she saw someone crying, she couldn't help but feel their sadness herself.

"Yayoi?" Someone called out from behind me. I turned and saw my sister. "Come for a walk with me. Mama needs to get things ready for us."

I nodded and stood up. My mother handed my sister some pocket money and told her to go get ourselves something nice. I remember the pattern on her purse: it was black, with small roses.

"Be back in time for our bentos," my mother said.

My father loved to buy boxed dinners from the department store deli counters, and always brought us back a selection. We'd light a lantern and have a picnic in the garden. He often fell asleep in the grass afterward. The three of us would carry him inside, or my mother would lay a mattress out for him, and either seemed to me like the pinnacle of fun. My sister would sometimes draw on his sleeping face mercilessly with a marker, but he'd only look in the mirror and beam, and never get angry at all. That was what he was like. He even got my sister back once by using a brush to draw a mustache on her face while she was asleep. That day, yes, he'd just bought a new car . . . That was why we'd decided to go on a trip.

In my dream, I identified completely with my childhood self. I was reliving the past just as it had happened. It flooded my chest, so familiar it made me want to cry.

That sunset was the reddest I'd ever seen.

The vermilion clouds coloring the autumn sky reached toward the buildings making up the horizon. My big sister took my hand and we went out through the wooden gate. The whole world seemed safe when I was with her. I felt like I could face anything. *Will you play piano for me later?* I said. I loved her playing. She smiled sweetly with the sunset behind her and the wind in her hair, and I entrusted my sorrow to her grown-up smile, the warmth of her hand.

Where was that house?

We reached an old shopping district. The stores lining its narrow streets were bustling in the evening hour. There was a fishmonger, a greengrocer, and a store selling dry goods, and a cacophony of different voices and smells all mixing together. I looked up at the throng and its blinding lights from a child's-eye view. Adults we knew called to us as we walked hand in hand. *Hi, Yukino! Hello, Yayoi!* Warm smiles and hands patting my head. I was tearful for no reason, and everyone was so kind.

There, in the midst of a beautiful evening, my heart must have been full of that premonition.

Because that was the last day our family ever spent in that neighborhood where we'd had such a blissful, happy life.

＊

By the time I got off the train at Noheji on the Tohoku Main Line and caught a taxi toward Osorezan, it was nearly night. I'd traveled so far since waking up that morning that all my senses felt numb, and I gazed out the window as everything I could see flitted past like a movie. The car wound its way higher and higher up the early summer mountain, giving me a beautiful view of the deepening color setting into the sky. It glowed clear and extended far into the distance beyond the green mountains.

The urgency of my need to find my aunt as soon as possible was quietly ebbing away into the landscape. Each bend the car made its way up, taking me deeper into the mountain as I leaned against the pull of the gradient, brought my certainty nearer. *She's close. I'm almost there.* My mind was strangely calm. Through the taxi window, the departing sun cast its last light across my hands, clasped on my lap, and everything seemed somehow very transparent.

Just then, the driver honked lightly. I looked up and saw a water fountain just ahead by the side of the road. And there next to it, somewhat anticlimactically, stood my aunt.

"What's that, there?" I asked.

"Spring water. Would you like to try it? It's good drinking, and cold," said the driver.

My aunt was taking big gulps of the water from the scoop, paying no attention to the car driving toward her. She stood there carelessly, her long dark blue skirt fluttering in the wind, empty-handed like she had just wandered out on a walk.

"Yes, could we stop here for a minute?" I said, and got out of the car.

The mountain air was cool. *There you are.*

My aunt noticed me straight away. She saw me coming up the road, put down the scoop of spring water she was about to pour into her hand, turned toward me, and smiled. It was a bewitching smile. She was more beautiful than I'd ever seen her. On that mountain path, with a cliffside at her back, she seemed to be breathing in our deep green surroundings. She looked free, and happy, even a little larger-than-life.

The wind blew, and with a smile that seemed to stop time, she said, "Yayoi. You came."

Her voice was sweet. "I wasn't sure how long I should stay."

I went up to her slowly and, blown by the same pleasant breeze, I looked into her eyes. We could hear the trickle of the spring flowing away past our feet.

"Get in the car with me, and let's go to Osorezan," I said. I pointed to the taxi waiting behind me.

My aunt nodded, and tilted the scoop she was holding, letting the water spill out slowly. Then she propped it back up against the fountain and started walking toward the taxi.

"You were sitting next to me like this that day, too," she said, sitting next to me in the back seat. Her eyes were as distant as a dream. "I can hardly believe it really happened."

"Were we supposed to go to Osorezan together?" I said.

"That's right. We never made it."

Her hair mostly hid her face from me, but I saw her lips form those tragic words. I could picture it now: our family in a car, driving up the mountain road just like this. Our mother and father in the front seats, the two of us in the back. Bumping and rumbling our way up the slope, we'd have been chatting away cheerfully until right before it happened. I remembered it clearly now. My father's soft, deep eyes, and the gentle slope of my mother's shoulders.

"Look. This is where it happened. Do you feel something?" My aunt smiled.

In a few seconds, the car had passed the spot. I said, "No, nothing," and smiled back at her.

I really didn't feel anything. I just saw how the mountains against the western sky glowed faintly green, and pale pink shadows lingered in the sky. It was a pretty view.

Leaving the taxi waiting by the red bridge at the edge of the lake, we made our way toward the entrance to the sacred site.

*

What had possessed them to visit the gates to the underworld on a family vacation? It was a truly bizarre landscape. It was as if we'd wandered into an alternate dimension. On each of the innumerable mounds that rose toward the sky stood multitudes of stone statues, silhouetted against the sweet blue of the evening. Countless stupas swayed, crows circled, and the smell of sulfur drifted pungently across the pale, desolate, weedless volcanic expanse.

I still couldn't believe that I'd found my aunt, and that she was here with me. We walked up the mountain, passing hundreds of statues on our way. Other walkers dotted the landscape, but from a distance they looked like toys among the rocks. An array of buildings cast their shadows on the dry, rough ground. The small statues that seemed to kneel by the path were wrapped with colorful scraps of cloth that made them look like people. Everywhere, stones had been piled up in unnatural forms, and everything was strangely silent. I felt like we were in a dreamscape. When I looked back over my shoulder, the green mountains seemed to loom behind me. We climbed up among great gray boulders, between jets of steam that erupted to our left and right. As we got higher, the sky grew dark and the view opened up. Finally, we reached the tall statue at the peak of the hill, and my aunt sat down on the ground by its feet.

"You always sit anywhere," I said, leaning against the statue. There must have been other things to talk about, but I couldn't bring myself to care. There with her in the cool air, looking out over the gray, oddly flattened landscape together, I was content.

"Of course. I like sitting, it's easy," my aunt said. The wind had blown her hair from her face, and I was reminded of what she'd looked like as a girl.

"Our mother and father—I remembered what they looked like," I said.

". . . Oh," she said.

Her gaze was soft. She was watching the crows fly away on slow black wings.

"I thought your brother might be with you," she said.

"This seemed like a place for blood relations only," I said, and laughed. "I was with him earlier. And that boy Masahiko."

"Oh! I was worried he'd come after me. I gave him the address, didn't I? Why did I do that?" She smiled a little.

"Do you like him?" I asked.

"I like him," she said.

"Then why are you avoiding him?"

"Say there's a wrestler you like. That doesn't mean you should be their manager."

"I don't think that's a fair comparison," I said. "He's not in high school anymore."

"No . . . But he was. When I met him. It was fun," she said

quietly, as if recollecting. "I was playing the piano to myself that day after school. I'd gotten engrossed, and then someone knocked on the door, and I realized it was totally dark outside. I said, 'Come in,' and it was him."

The horizon was adorned with the last remains of the light, and layers of indigo darkened the sky. Over the otherworldly landscape before us, shadow was falling.

"I liked the way he looked, so I used to watch him. And I liked his singing voice. We went out for tea, and he scared me by telling me about the school's seven mysteries . . . Then he said he'd walk me home, so we went through the park. He kissed me out of nowhere in the dark among the plants, and said he liked me."

"I've never heard anything like it," I said, astonished. It was an incredible thing for him to have done.

Dreamily, my aunt went on, "I was so happy. Because I liked his face. Yes, that was the start of it."

"But you can't go back?" I asked, again.

"That's what I thought. It felt all wrong somehow. But not anymore. I'm here with my sister," she said, standing up. "I've seen the view I was supposed to see years ago. I wasn't hung up on it, really, but I feel better now. I even feel like I might want to patch things up with him."

I thought of Masahiko's smile. We'd only just met, but over curry and beer and train rides, I felt like I'd gotten to know him.

"Come on, Yayoi. Let's go down to the lake. That part of the shore's called Paradise Beach."

She started walking, and I followed.

At the bottom of the long sloping path, we came to an old temple hall where a large stone statue stood in the shadow of great piles of clothes, toys, and paper cranes. My aunt stopped for a second and peered at the statue standing there, its eyes closed peacefully. She jingled around in her pocket, pulled out a coin, and threw it toward the statue. Then, raising one hand toward her face as if to say sorry, she walked on. Seeing me looking a question at her with my eyes, she smiled a little.

"You know, don't you? About the baby," she said. "That was the biggest thing—why I didn't think I could stay with him."

Against the backdrop of the mountains, the deep blue lake stood quietly, full of clear water. Suddenly, we were stepping not across rock, but fine white sand that seemed to float dimly against the evening sky. The landscape opened up, and only the stacked stones remained to remind us of hell.

"It really is as beautiful and silent as paradise," I said.

It was a lonely sight. There was almost something holy about it. The silent open shore, and the cold wind that blew across it, and the water of the lake susurrating at its edge. The first star of the evening gleamed in the light of the far sky. The darkness was creeping in, obscuring my aunt's features. But she was here, by my side, offering up a quiet prayer toward this beautiful sight, just like me.

"It's been so long," she said, softly.

It's finally over, I thought. My heart felt like it had been washed clean.

"Thanks for coming so quickly. I admire your initiative," she said. She was looking at the water lapping at the shore, her lashes lowered. She pushed her hair out of her face with fingers that looked identical to mine. "I see now I was always thinking about you, even when it didn't seem like I was," she said. "I'm so glad you remembered."

"I feel like I've been with you this whole time," I said.

My aunt looked at me with a smile in her eyes, and chuckled.

"Don't give me that. I know you were with your brother," she said.

Yes, I'd been with Tetsuo, too. We'd taken a journey together as if we'd just woken up from a long dream.

"True," I said, nodding. "It was only for a few days, but they were pretty special."

They really had been—extraordinary, singular, priceless.

"What a trip," my aunt said. "Well, I'll be okay now. So you can go home, too, Yayoi."

"I will," I said.

I was going home. Nothing about the real issue had been resolved; in fact, I knew there were only more challenges waiting up ahead. Each one would need to be overcome, by me, but also by Tetsuo. And they'd be difficult, perhaps nearly insurmountable. But there was still nowhere else for me to call home; I'd seen for myself how fate worked. And yet nothing had been taken away, only given. I hadn't lost my aunt and my brother—no, by taking matters into my own hands, I'd discovered my sister, and my sweetheart.

The wind picked up. Darkness overtook the sky like a slow velvet curtain falling, and the stars started to twinkle; first one, then another, and another.

Looking out over the dark lake, almost as if we were hoping to catch a glimpse of our lost family drifting somewhere across it, Yukino and I stood there together in silence for a little while longer.